# THE SERPENT AMONGST
# THE LILIES

# The
# Serpent Amongst
# the Lilies

P. C. DOHERTY

St. Martin's Press
New York

Library of Congress Cataloging-in-Publication Data

Doherty, P. C.
    The serpent amongst the lilies / P. C. Doherty.
      p.   cm.
    ISBN 0-312-05154-9
    I. Title.
PR6054.037S47   1990
823'.914—dc20                                         90-37295
                                                     CIP


First published in Great Britain by Robert Hale Limited

First U.S. Edition
10  9  8  7  6  5  4  3  2  1

To my Mother, Catherine, who introduced
me to the joy of studying history

# ONE

They always said I would hang, finish my life at the end of a rope swinging from some scaffold. Perhaps even the Elms in London. Dancing there, black-faced, eyes staring, my corpse given up to the crows. They were wrong. Some of those who prophesied my fate died just as violently on the battlefield, their sleek, soft flesh shattered by lance, mace or sword. Or, because of their treasonable conspiracies, on a scaffold set up in some market-town while the peasants and burgesses stood round and laughed to see such great ones brought low. But not Jankyn.

I, Matthew Jankyn, Lord of the Manor of Newport in Shropshire, with its granges, fields, meadows, fisheries, carp-ponds, stews, now lie in my great four-poster bed between silk sheets. I tell my story to this little whey-faced clerk who writes it down. I know the mouldy bastard does not like me and he certainly does not like the story I tell, but who cares what he thinks? I have never liked priests with their pious, white faces, fat bellies and stumbling ways. I've always said that once you have met one you have met the lot. I can see from the little bastard's eyes how he does not like that. If he is not careful, I will pick up my stick and beat him on the knuckles. After all, why should he complain? I have given him a living, haven't I? He has access to my table, my pantry, my buttery and, above all, my beautiful sack and burgundy. I still drink deep draughts despite what the doctor said with all his physics, horoscopes and mutterings. I hate priests. Doctors come a good second. They thrive on human pain, charge high fees and do nothing. If I had my way, I would hang the lot alongside lawyers. I know they, too, are waiting for me to die.

Yet here I am, Matthew Jankyn, professional soldier, knight, war-hero, but only I know the truth. Jankyn is a coward who has survived on his wits. I am now ninety years of age but I still ask for a young, lissome girl to warm my sheets at night. During the days I spend most of my time ignoring the doctor's predictions and the priest's admonitions by drinking sack until I fall into a drunken stupor, for, as I say, who cares? I have seen the world. I have seen the stars and planets wheel above this vale of tears. Now they say I am at death's door but what do they know? If I go, who cares? Matilda, my only true love, she surely would plead for me with the good Christ, for I have done terrible wrong? However, I have also tried, in my own way, to do some good. I am always kind to my neighbour, even though I may try to seduce his wife. I have drunk too much but I have never stopped anyone else drinking. I look after my peasants, though I chase their daughters. I have hurt no man, unless attacked. But I babble on. You don't want to listen to this, but to my past stirring times! I suppose, as you get older, your mind wanders back to youthful days. Now, brain-sick, I think of the days when my uncaked blood in all its channels flowed like wine from a new bottle. And the memories? Birds scuffling in the bushes. A gust of birds across golden harvest fields. Swallows skimming across the haze of the lake and green soft rushes talking to the wind which lulls them to sleep.

Yet you are not interested in these memories, but in the terrors! Satan saying his matins at midnight. Towns, palaces, houses roaring red to heaven. Men in glittering armour, all iron and lightning, as they stride through cobbled streets drenched with blood to drain their loins on some young maiden's. Savage pursuits through barbaric forests, meshes of branch and root. Cold days, the grass heavy with water, on the wild moors of France and England. I have seen battlefields with the flesh piled high as in a butcher's store, steaming and glistening under a drenching sun. Fields sodden with blood. Whole armies facing each other like caged panthers, the devil stoking their eyes with hate, prepared to kill and hack each other. Oh yes, I have seen such days.

Shadows scudding across my soul. Generals, whores, courtesans, young girls in Venus' clothing with soft flesh and perfumed skin. Silken sheets and the most expensive, fragrant, tasty wines cooling in iced waters. The blast of trumpets with bedecked blazons, the sound of drum and pipe as men prepare to kill each other, still wake me after the chimes of midnight. I lie and remember, the peasant's hovel, the turreted hall, the sharp blade shearing, shattering the bone and sinking deep into sleek, soft flesh. I feel hungry and recall the banquets with all varieties of meat and minstrelsy in the swept, tapestried, voluptuous halls of power. Yet I cannot forget the hedgerows, rank and rich, where I have hidden while men better than I have tried to kill me; going through towns littered with refuse, stinking of every stale odour under the sun; or, half slain by sleet and snow, crossing valleys and high hills which peer over forests of heavy oaks, birds singing on their bleak branches, crooning themselves to sleep under a dying sun.

Images. They come and go and dash like flying shadows across my brain. At night they all come back and when I am dead I will join them, for sleep, as the philosopher says, is but the image of death. I just wish I could impose some order.

The young girl with her young, proud breasts

hand-cupped, and above her some horrid weapon swinging savagely down to split us both. Arrows shooting through the shimmering air, and the ghastly fear of ghoulish ghosts who, when I am alone here, come back tripping up the broad-beamed oak staircase to stand, a silent array, an army, a phalanx, round my bed.

Matilda never comes but Beaufort is there. Cardinal, politician, banker, saint or arch-devil, I never knew. He is always there with his olive skin, angel mouth and devil eyes. Dressed in purple and scarlet with white gloves. One of his hands always fingering the beautiful, jewel-encrusted pectoral cross on his chest. He looks at me reproachfully, wondering why I am lying here when I should be in France. Beaufort, illegitimate son of John of Gaunt, with his pretensions to the throne and ambitions to become Pope. A clever, saturnine man who could have outwitted Reynard the fox. Cunning, devious, brilliant, charming, cruel, gentle, hard and vicious. Every time I see the beautiful bastard, I think of France. It was not like it is now, a great nation under formidable kings. Oh no, in my youth France was England's battleground and a playground for Henry V, my noble, vicious hawk of a king and his quarrelsome arrogant generals; Talbot; Beauchamp, Earl of Warwick; Montague, Earl of Salisbury. Above all, John, Duke of Bedford, silver-haired, caring, courteous and determined to bring half of France under the orbit of an infant king who was more sane when he was a child than when he was a man. But I prattle on. Let me explain.

I was born in Shropshire, raised here, went to Oxford and became a scholar learning grammar, rhetoric, theology, philosophy, studying the masters, Abelard, Bernard, Aristotle and Plato. There, I fell from grace, linked to the Whyte Harte, the cause which espoused poor, dead Richard II who was deposed by Henry,

Duke of Lancaster, in 1399. Richard was imprisoned in Pontefract but his cause stirred men up. The Whyte Harte, Richard's personal emblem, was used by traitors, evil men like Sir John Oldcastle. God, how I hated him! Because of him, the cause was betrayed, Matilda went mad and I spent years in Beaufort's service who used me as a spy to track down the truth as well as find Oldcastle. I did both and had the satisfaction of seeing Oldcastle's body explode lashed to a barrel in Smithfield, watching the flames eat his fat, rotting corpse and shatter his evil, plotting brain. Beaufort then sent me to France where I fought for Henry V, victor of Agincourt, shatterer of armies and conquerer of France. God, how Henry loved killing. He swept round Normandy, burning, pillaging and, with his troops, taking anything which moved, and burning what they could not. Grand lads and grand generals. They have gone to their just deserts. I will probably meet them all in hell.

You see, Henry V came to the throne in 1413, fourteen years after his father had snatched the English throne from Richard. However, that didn't bother our young Henry, the noble lord. He smashed his enemies at home and, taking the title King of France, led his armies across the Channel and began the great adventure in the autumn of 1415. I was with his army, by compulsion of course, having never volunteered for anything in my life. I always accepted the proverb that 'he who volunteers never lives to pay-day'. Yet I was at Agincourt when our bowmen sent clouds of flying death into the French chivalry, decimating them. King Henry used that victory to march on Paris and the real war began. France could not resist. Its king, Charles VI, was imbecilic, insane, drooling in his dirty chambers and worrying about what to do while his wife, Isabeau of Bavaria, collected her menagerie around her. Not only of animals but anyone who fell low enough to become her lover. The blessed offspring of this precious pair, the Dauphin Charles, was no better. Knock-kneed and with a shambling gait, thin-faced, long-nosed, a mouth which always hung open (with the liquids from both mouth and nose staining the front of his jerkin). He was not exactly the sort of prince to stimulate interest or loyalty from those who followed him.

At the time, France was not so much alive but a great, rotting corpse, its only life being the maggots which ate away at it. The maggots were two great armies. The Armagnacs under the Dauphin and the Burgundians under their powerful Duke John. They fought each other with a savagery which even astonished the English and refused to unite against the threat posed by Henry and his wandering, marauding armies. In 1418, the Burgundians and Armagnacs agreed to a meeting on the Bridge of Montereau which spanned the river Yonne. Burgundy was prepared to make his peace, kneeling at the feet of the Dauphin and the other Armagnac generals, but the Dauphin gave a sign and the Duke was hacked to death. Because of his death, the English armies managed to conquer most of northern France, for the powerful Burgundian faction joined Henry. They declared eternal war on the Dauphin, accepting Henry's claim to be crowned in Paris and proclaimed as King of France.

The terror began. No wonder the French called us 'Gondons' or 'Goddamns'. Years ago, I read a dialogue between France and Truth written by some moralist. (You know the type, men who like to keep comfortable and write theses about morality. It is easy for them. How can you be virtuous if you have never been tempted?) My scribe, this little mouse of a priest, is looking strangely at me so I think I should ignore such moral reflections and continue. The war the English have waged and still wage (claims France in this dialogue) is false, treacherous and damnable. But then again, the

English are an accursed race, opposed to all good and all reason; ravening wolves; proud, arrogant, hypocrites, tricksters without any conscience; tyrants and persecutors of Christians, men who drink and gorge on human blood, with natures like birds of prey, people like wolves who live only by plunder. This was a Frenchman's view of the English. Believe me, it is an understatement.

The English armies marched through France taking their banners up to the walls of Paris and on 1st September 1420, King Henry, Philip of Burgundy and Charles VI made a ceremonial entry into Paris. The banners flew and the trumpets brayed and shrieked, their crack stilling the roar of the crowd. The Te Deum was sung by priests and everyone came to hail Henry as Charles' legitimate successor to the crown of France. Henry spent Christmas in the Louvre Palace being courted by poor Charles who, on many occasions, failed to recognise him. Charles' overblown, blowsy queen, with her monkeys and dogs climbing over everything, dirtying them with their shit, cheerfully proclaimed to the world that her own son, the Dauphin, was, in fact, a bastard, the illegitimate issue of one of her many affairs. While Henry stayed in the Louvre, garbed in silk, eating swan, venison, boar, carp, salmon, and gulping down the best from France's vineyards, the situation in Paris was horrific. The city rubbish-tips were filled with the bodies of little children who died looking for something to eat amongst the refuse. The people began to devour swill and filth even the lean-flanked pigs in the streets would not touch. Wolves came out of the eastern forests and swam the Seine to disinter and gnaw at the newly-buried corpses. Yet Henry and his commanders rode the streets of Paris, their proud heads held high like stags.

So Henry was proclaimed Charles VI's heir and married the mad king's daughter, Katherine, a small, winsome, black-haired, alabaster-skinned beauty. Henry proposed that the issue of the marriage would be king of England and France. He set to with gusto so that his bride's cries and shrieks during love-making could often be heard throughout the palace. Henry had his way and little Katherine became pregnant. Henry, of course, was as romantic as he could be in the circumstances, openly apologising for spending most of his honeymoon besieging the city of Sens. Meanwhile, the poor Dauphin retreated to the city of Bourges and waited for God to give a sign. He did whilst Henry was in England. The King's impulsive brother, Clarence, (who was a fierce young falcon of a boy and jealous of his brother), decided he, too, could win victories in France. On Easter Sunday, he was at dinner in Pont de l'Arche in Normandy (after he had returned from his usual pastime of raiding and ravishing beyond the Marne) when he heard a French army was in the vicinity. Clarence, refusing to wait for archers who were the spine and the arm of the English army, galloped off with over one thousand men-at-arms. He met the enemy, crossed a river and charged them uphill (like the idiot he was), forcing his horsemen over boggy ground. The Armagnacs sat there and watched in astonishment and then, led by a Scots force (who, as usual, were fighting for anyone who paid) under the Earl Buchan, counter-charged and beat the English back to the river. Clarence, easily seen by the royal colours wrapped round his chest and the coronet on his helmet, was pulled off his horse. He was beaten to death, his body stripped and tossed in a cart to be taken for the Dauphin to view. It was only rescued by the Earl of Salisbury who came up to save the survivors and take back Clarence's battered corpse to England.

In June 1421, Henry landed in France and, eager to avenge his brother's death, went on a wave of killing and slaughter. At one castle he stormed, he hanged all the Scots. Their French commander, whom Henry was also going to hang, protested that, as he had once fought for Henry, he was a comrade-at-arms and, according to the rules of chivalry, could not be executed. Henry grudgingly agreed but hanged him up in an iron, rusting cage from the castle wall! When he took the Armagnac castle of Rougement, he executed the entire garrison, demolishing the building and drowning the defenders. He crossed the Marne and marched on the city of Meaux, and, in the most rain-swept of autumns, brought up his cannon and began to mine and bombard the walls. The ground was waterlogged with rains and floods. A sharp frost set in and both English and French started dying like flies on a cold summer's day. Not because of any fighting but because of disease, in particular dysentery. Henry, himself, became ill but was encouraged by the news that on the 6th of December Queen Katherine had, at last, borne the fruit of his rough love-making and given birth to a son and heir at Windsor. Then, it was a cause of great rejoicing. Now, years later, looking down the arch of time, I realise that the poor sod born at Windsor may have been Henry's son but he was also the grandson of Charles VI of France and inherited most of his grandfather's madness as well as a good strain of sanctity. By the way, the gloomy legend 'Henry born at Monmouth shall small time reign and get much and Henry born at Windsor shall long reign and lose all' was not said at the time but came years later. In fact, I coined it, being clever at a banquet, but that is another story. What concerns us now is something beyond the span of life and time, divine intervention or witchcraft, I do not know which. I did say I have seen Satan singing matins at midnight. It is really worse than that for I have actually knelt alongside him.

Oh, where was I? I rattle on and the smug little clerk is sitting there trying to pretend he has not farted. I am too tired and too drunk to beat him but I will remember it tomorrow. Anyway, where was I? Oh yes, at Meaux with Henry. He captured the town, you know, in March 1422 because he took his artillery on to an island in the river, built wooden shelters and battered the walls, relentlessly, until the garrison had to lay down its arms and sue for unconditional surrender. The commander, a bastard, was hanged from a tree where he had gibbeted his own victims. Henry completed his chivalrous treatment by beheading the body as well as that of a trumpeter who had jeered at him. Some of the other defenders who had mocked him by beating a donkey on the walls until it brayed, and claimed it was King Henry calling them, were confined for life in some of France's nastiest prisons. The rest of the captives, men, women and children, together with cartloads of booty, were sent back to England.

But Henry's time had come. His bowels were rotting and his innards turned to water. In August, he was taken back to the castle of Vincennes to die. Henry really thought he was going to heaven. Yet, as he lay there, in his own muck and dirt, some demon or devil or maybe the ghastly ghosts of those he had sent to a horrid death, congregated round his bed. Suddenly he sat up straight, shouting at the darkness.

'You lie! You lie! My portion is with the Lord Jesus Christ.'

Then he died, leaving France and England to a puny, puking little boy.

# TWO

I suppose when the lion is dead the hawks gather, and so it was after Henry V's death. First, there was Gloucester who was arrogant, cocky, with all his brother's ambition but very little of his talent. There were some good generals: Beauchamp, Earl of Warwick, with the face of a saint and the mind and manners of a drunken Mongol; John, Duke of Bedford, the cautious, diplomatic general and administrator, Regent of France and England, a more sophisticated and cultured man than his dead brother but just as ruthless. He was aided and abetted by two beauties. Thomas Montague, Earl of Salisbury, a very strict warrior who specialised in cannons and bombards as well as dragging his prisoners back to Paris at the end of a rope; and the man I have mentioned, Richard Beauchamp, Earl of Warwick, Captain of Calais, Rouen, Meaux and Beauvais. This unholy trinity at war, Bedford, Salisbury and Warwick, were aided and abetted by other goshawks, falcons of the same hue. Lord Talbot, Lord Scales, Sir John Falstaff (a great thief, him), William Glasdale, and, at home, my own Lord and Master, Henry Beaufort, Bishop of Winchester and Cardinal of England.

I had left Beaufort's service two years before Henry's death. I had broken the treason of the Whyte Harte, found the truth about Richard's death and brought my own enemies to destruction. I had acquired substantial lands, wealth, and bags of gold put away like salted meat with merchants and bankers in London. I also had letters of pardon and warrants from Beaufort to acquire back the lands my father had forfeited while dying bleakly, a black bundle on white snow, in Richard's cause decades earlier. However, I had lost my only love, Matilda, and I had had enough of war. I let others serve with Henry's armies in France for I had seen the killing and it sickened me. There are other ways for a man to acquire wealth and I used my bags of gold to do this. I bought back my father's land, clearing the hedgerows, rebuilding the manor and making sure my peasants worked hard. I cheated my officials but ensured they didn't cheat the peasants. I became accustomed to the quiet tenor of country life, with the annual routine of the year; the accounts of spring, midsummer and Michaelmas, together with the division of land, purpestures, assarts, common fields, field strips, messuages, charters, rolls and manor courts.

I redecorated the church of St. Mary in the village of Newport. Every Sunday I rode down like a king in his own realm to sit in the most important pew before the chancel screen to listen to Father William preach. I would always ride slowly through the winding streets which ran from the church like spokes from the centre of a wheel, inspecting each of the houses. Some were neat and trim with thatched roofs and in good repair and others delapidated, showing evident signs of decay and neglect. This was usually due to the fact that the man of the family was either dead or missing in the wars. I always inspected my real enemies, the prosperous peasants and villeins in their larger houses. These were situated a little back from the lanes so that the ground around them was roughly enclosed with a wicker fence and filled with young cabbage, onions, parsley, leeks and a few herbs. At the bottom of these gardens were the boundaries, which were a constant cause of enmity. I was very strict in ensuring they did not encroach on any land belonging to me.

Whenever I passed the battered stone cross (and God knows who placed it there), I blessed myself with every sign of reverence so that the women looked at me slant-eyed and whispered how good and pious a man I was. Oh, I think they knew the truth. They were not as stupid as they appeared. They knew I liked a pretty face and a comely figure and any maid saucy enough would always catch my eye. Sometimes, out of boredom, I would dismount and enter one of my tenants' houses, watching the women fan the embers from the previous night's fire before hanging a large metal pot of water over it. They would rearrange the beds, sweep the floor with a besom of large twigs and set out the trestle-table with bread and milk upon it. After which, the great chest in the corner of the main room of the house was opened and the coloured dresses and bright clothes they wore on Sundays and festivals would be laid out.

The bell of the church would ring. I would walk with the family along the narrow, rutted track to the church clucking my tongue at the graveyard wall which had decayed in some places, noting how pigs and sheep had wandered in to graze amongst the tombs. I would assure all, with careful nod and narrow eye, how I would later have a word with the priest. And so into the church and down to my special pew before the chancel screen. This would be the sign for Father William to come in and begin the Mass. I, thoughtful as any angel carved by a sculptor, would kneel on my own prie-dieu with hands joined and eyes heavenwards. When I thought nobody was looking, I did scan the church for who was missing or, more importantly, any new, pretty face. Soon, Father William began his sermon and the peasants squatted in the rushes in the nave of the church or leaned against pillars wishing for him to finish. I would hear his opening words which were usually some

reference to the Old Testament about Elias or Elijah.
(God knows why these priests seem to like the Old
Testament when the New Testament is one of love!)
Anyway, I would look at the stained-glass window I had
bought for the church and then up at a painting (which
was my favourite one, strangely enough) of the Last
Judgement – Christ in majesty with a set of scales and,
on either side, the souls of the just and wicked. The
damned interested me with their look of absolute
astonishment, the depravity, the naked women, (for I
had had the painting commissioned), and the devils
many of whom I had given the faces of people I knew at
court. I had thought of putting Beaufort in but realised
he would be out of place. If Beaufort joined Satan's
camp, he would be a Prince of Devils and not some little
imp with a fork waiting for a commonplace lecher like
myself to fall into his hands. After Father William shut
up, I would listen to the rest of the Mass, paying
attention when the Christ became present under the
bread and the blood – I always took the sacrament as
worthily as I could. Once Father William had intoned
the 'Ita Missa est', I would rise, bow to the altar and walk
down the church as grand as any pope in his palace.

I became accustomed to the life of the manor. I
attended the court, checking with my stewards and
bailiffs, beadles and reeves; I would ride out to the
outlying granges, fields and meadows, protecting my
villagers from the tax-gatherers who moved like a
colony of ants from village to village exacting what they
could. I always resisted them, flourishing warrants from
Beaufort, dropping names and hinting that I, too, had
powerful friends at Court and it was best if they moved
on. Still, I do not think the villagers liked me. They saw
me for what I was, a man who liked his own comfort, his
own wines and any pretty woman ready to warm his
bed. In the main, I left them alone and I think they
respected me. I set up a three-branched gallows at a

crossroads outside the village, though I only hanged one, a man who had abducted a young girl, abused her and burnt her feet over coals before raping her. My bailiffs caught him and I hauled him before the manor court and had him hanged. The King's Justices, when they came round on their circuit, protested, but I didn't give a fig for them. Once again, I talked ominously of writing to my Lord Beaufort. The conversation dried up and the Judges moved on to take bribes and execute the law in other parts.

I spent most of my money and my wealth building and redecorating the great Manor House. I call it great and I suppose it was, with its own herb and rose gardens, stables, forges and barns. They clustered around the main house built over cold, stone cellars which held (and still do) a fine collection of wines. I had travelled both in France and England visiting the opulent palaces of King Henry and his nobles so I knew what I wanted: a chimneyed hearth built in the main room where charcoal burned, my own ornately carved chair placed cunningly before it, gorgeously bedecked with cushions in quilted work and cunningly embroidered. It was covered with a magnificent mantle, maroon in colour, made from the finest fabric and lined with fur and ermine. I bought silken bedding for my own chamber and curtains brilliant with bright gold hems, skilfully-sewn coverlets with comely panels and fringes made out of the costliest fur and adorned with red-gold rings and cords. Tapestries of Toulouse silk and precious stuffs from Turkestan covered both floor and walls. In my hall, I set up trestle-tables covered with brilliant white cloths where my guests were royally hosted by servants who had washed their hands and wore clean garb. I hired the finest cooks who served appetising soups, lavishly-seasoned fish in all its kinds with some baked in bread, some browned on coals, some broiled, other served with spice but always subtly sauced as a man likes it. Good Lord, by God's bones, I loved my food almost as I did the pleasures of the bed, Once or twice, I brought a young courtesan from London and, on one occasion, from France. They served me and my visitors well in bed. I tried to look at the good in it. At least they kept me away from the village maidens.

The years elapsed. The seasons passed. The wheel turned. I attended the court, the church, the feasting and the revelry within the village, birth and marriage ceremonies, funerals and baptisms. Some children were named after me, a few out of reverence but many made the father or suspicious husband wonder how the child was engendered. Yet I was a good lord, though a bored one. Perhaps this kept me alert and always looking south towards France, listening for the tidbits of news brought by pedlars, journeymen and merchants. Of course I made the odd journey to London when I wanted to. I always stayed away from the messy, murky politics of the city but I kept myself informed about the horrors happening in France after Henry's death.

The Regent Bedford proved to be an able commander and tactful diplomat. Still, the killing continued as he tried to drive the Dauphin's forces out of northern France. In this he was aided and abetted by Burgundy, for Bedford had married Anne, the Duke's sister. It was a political match which also happened to be a remarkably happy one. The English and Burgundians fielded common armies and old Salisbury proved his worth. On one occasion, even though it was so hot the English men-at-arms lay in their armour face down on the ground to cool off, Salisbury brought the French to battle and defeated them. I saw some of the fruits of this victory even in Shropshire, the jewels, money, booty and plunder brought back by local lords who had raised their companies and taken them to war. But there were other signs, like rags blowing in the wind. Soldiers returning from France, wounded, dismembered and suffering terrible hardship. I remember one winter, I think it must have been 1428. The snow fell, covering the fields and moors of Shropshire. So bitterly cold, even the great hare on the hill sat shivering with clenched teeth under a bush and birds froze in the branches. My bailiff woke me one morning and took me down to see a horrid sight. In one of our barns, we found three men in rags, their faces dirty. They had frozen to death clinging to each other for warmth. Such a piteous death. I only wished I had seen them first. I cannot stand misery. It only upsets me and disturbs my own comfort. I gave the three bodies burial and warned my tenants not to listen to the Commissioners of Array. However, when the Commissioners came through with trumpet, fife and tambour to beat up support to follow the banners to France, there were always fools ready enough to kiss their parents, wives or daughters goodbye and go swinging down some leafy lane. Most of them never returned.

The war continued with terrible ferocity, with each side beheading hostages and showing no mercy. In fact, they made compacts that until the final victory was decided no prisoners would be taken.

The troops which poured across to France often took the law into their own hands and set up independent companies called 'Ecorcheurs' or 'Flayers'. They earned their name from their vile acts of robbery: they stripped their victims to the skin and often flayed them alive, pinning the skins to the church door or trees as a warning against any retaliation.

I was tempted to join these forces and restore my fortunes by some quick plunder in France but I suppose I am a born coward. The prospect of campaigning in the mud of Normandy, even for a bucket of jewels or heavy ransom, daunted me. After all, it would mean fighting. I had a very keen sense of my own survival and wished to keep my skin. Moreover, I was in pursuit of a pretty young widow from the village of Drayton who resisted my advances with pretty pleas and murmurs about morality. Oh Lord, a full eighteen months to bring her to bed, but then she sang a different song. I remember her well not because she was special but my amorous designs coincided with the rumours sweeping into London and through the countryside. How the French had acquired a new leader, an extraordinary person, a young maid from Lorraine who had appeared before the Dauphin and promised that she would lead his armies to victory and take him to Rheims to be crowned like his predecessors. She was called La Pucelle, the Maid, but the English called her the Limb of Satan, a sorceress, a witch, someone who dabbled in the black arts. I could well believe such stories; even in my small comfortable nook of the world the forces of darkness and the adoration of Satan were not unknown. To the west lay the great forests of Wales. People from my own village often went there to practise secret rites in ancient groves. I was still wondering about these stories at the start of 1429 when a messenger arrived at my manor wearing Beaufort's colours and carrying a simple message. The Cardinal wished, nay ordered me, to meet him in his manor of Cattehall in Essex as speedily as possible. I did not need a further bidding. I summoned my bailiffs and reeves. I left them careful instructions on the management and administration of my affairs, and bade a quick farewell. Haste was essential. Beaufort was not a man to be ignored. Moreover, the young widow was becoming rather importunate in her pleas, solicitations and hints as to how we might resolve our state by holy matrimony. In my life I have been threatened and cursed. I have fought in pitched battles and hidden in cold woods but nothing, and I repeat, nothing, (and never mind the priests and particularly the one who is writing my story) nothing holds as many horrors for me as the state of matrimony.

# THREE

I left Shropshire as I had arrived, riding a good steady horse with a sumpter pony on a lead carrying most of my treasured belongings. I travelled south-east along the old Roman road leading to London, enjoying the bright clear spring with its hard morning frosts and icy-blue skies at night. It was the first time I had travelled for years and I saw the changes caused by Henry's wars in France. Some of the villages were in a state of decay. In others, great fields lay untended displaying very little preparation for the spring sowing. The roads seemed clustered with beggars, landless vagabonds owing allegiance to no man. At every crossroads, there were scaffolds and it was rare to see one bare of its grisly blackening burden. I, a born rogue, felt a sense of sin, of growing evil and malevolence throughout the whole country. The wandering bands did not disturb me. I was well-armed and usually I travelled with a convoy of merchants, peasants going to London, travellers who were too powerful a group to attack. Now and again, however, we saw the effects of disorder, a body half-buried in a ditch and corpses bobbing amongst the reeds of some stream with their heads down and cruel purple wounds in their naked backs.

I considered ignoring Beauforts's summons and entering the capital to see what was happening and sample its pleasures. I could wander around Southwark, visiting different taverns, tasting the ale and buying hot pies or cherries fresh off the branch. I resisted the temptation and made direct along rutted tracks to the royal manor of Cattehall on the north-east of the city near the great forest of Epping. Thus, a week after I had left Shropshire, I entered the manor courtyard. Beaufort's retainers, resplendent in their livery, ran forward to take my horse, offer me wine and take me to a warm chamber to await His Eminence.

The Cardinal's house was a splendid affair. A walled courtyard enclosed stables, forges, herb gardens and banks of earth which, in the summer, would yield the most fragrant roses and flowers. Inside, the whole house centred round a beautiful oak-panelled hall with a hooded, canopied fireplace. The room was vaulted and the walls were covered with the most costly of silks and drapes. On the floor there were not rushes or straw but thick carpets woven in an intricate design of varying hues of purple and gold. Everywhere, on shelves, dressers and tables, winked silver and gold goblets, plates, dishes and spoons which were all symbols of the Bishop's wealth. Above the fireplace were the royal arms of England with a black bar across, signifying Beaufort was descended from royal blood, albeit illegitimately. I was given a small chamber above stairs which was warm, clean and whitewashed with lime. The floor was covered with thick soft rugs and there was a small four-poster bed covered with tasselled cord drapes. A jug of wine was cooling in ice-cold water and, surrounding it, goblets on a silver tray and dishes of sweetmeats. The Bishop may have been a man of God but he was equally aware of the comforts of this life.

The next morning, I met the Bishop, His Eminence Cardinal Henry Beaufort. He was waiting for me, seated in the great chair before the fireplace in his hall as if the ten years since our last meeting had vanished in the twinkling of an eye. He did not seem to have aged,

apart from the white streaks in his jet-black hair and
wrinkles around the eyes and mouth in his olive-
skinned face. The eyes were as dark and haunting as
ever, with the face as beautiful as an angel etched on a
tapestry. He had the same fluidity and elegance of
movement which always fascinated me. He offered me a
purple-gloved hand, adorned with the costliest of rings,
to kiss. I did, smelling the fragrant perfume from his
clothes, before he waved me to a seat opposite and
served me himself with cool, sweet, white wine and
paper-thin biscuits. They tasted of almond and melted
most deliciously in the mouth. I still remember the
scene for it is imprinted upon my brain like a seal on red
wax: the beautiful, sumptuous hall and Beaufort
opposite me smiling as if he knew my private thoughts
while making idle conversation about what had
happened over the years. Our relationship was hard to
define. We were friends, master and servant, enemies
and allies. We knew each other's secrets. I think he had
some respect for me. I know, and God is my witness, he
is the only man I really feared. After listening to me for
a while, Beaufort led the conversation round to the war
in France. I knew this lay at the heart of his summons to
me. He put his cup down and, cradling his hands in his
lap, looked wistfully at a point above my head.

'Jankyn,' he began. 'You have been, and perhaps still
are, one of my most faithful retainers and a rogue with a
stronge sense of survival. If you do not hang, I believe
you will live to die at a ripe old age in something akin to
the odour of sanctity. Possibly go to heaven to be the
least deserving fruit of Christ's redemption.' Looking
back, I think the bastard was right and perhaps, who
knows, I may end my days, my portion, with Christ
rather than the lord Satan with whom I have walked for
most of my life. 'Anyway,' His Eminence continued,
'you have heard of the situation in France?' I nodded.
'And about the Maid?'

'You mean La Poucelle, Jehanne D'Arc,' I replied. 'What about her? They say she is a witch.'

Beaufort nodded and pursed his lips before looking at me directly. 'And what if we are wrong?' he began smoothly, his voice silken yet still menacing as if I was personally responsible for the Maid. 'And what if we are wrong?' the Bishop continued. 'What happens if our situation is like that of Pilate and Herod who condemned someone whom history later judged to be sent directly by God. What then, Jankyn?'

I shrugged. 'What does it matter to me, my Lord? I am not there. Her blood, when she dies, will not be on my hands or yours.'

The Bishop nodded. 'But what happens if we prove Jehanne's claims to be a saint, to be God's own envoy on earth, a peasant girl raised by him to deliver France, are correct? What then, Jankyn?'

My heart sank a little for I knew what was coming next. 'My Lord,' I replied, 'I ask you again. What does it matter to you or I who Jehanne is?'

Beaufort leaned across and smiled, his eyes full of merriment as he tapped me gently on the knee. 'But what happens if only us two know, Jankyn?' He added, 'What happens if we gather the knowledge and build up a separate picture?'

'Look, my Lord,' I replied, 'we have done business before. I trust you as much as you trust me.' I watched the smile flit across Beaufort's face like a cloud scurrying across the face of the sun. 'I know what you are going to ask me, my Lord,' I continued, 'so why not ask and have done with it?'

Beaufort steepled his silk, purple-clad fingers resting his elbows on the heavy carved arms of the chair. 'This is my proposition, Jankyn,' he began smoothly. 'You are to go to France, to spy on Jehanne D'Arc's claims. You are to make enquiries. You are to gather information and send all of it to me.' The Bishop lifted an admonitory finger. 'It may well be that Jehanne is a witch and a sorceress and deserves to die.' The Bishop made a grimace with his lips. 'But it may be we are wrong and such knowledge would be interesting. It would be power.'

'My Lord,' I replied. 'Why ask me? You are Bishop of Winchester and a Cardinal. You could send your own public envoys to gather this information.'

'If I could do that, Jankyn,' he replied testily, 'then I would do it, but I cannot. That is why I am sending you.' He lifted a hand. 'Look, I know you are now a wealthy landowner, but your rents are low and your treasure has dwindled.' He continued earnestly, 'If you do this, Jankyn, there is wealth beyond your imagination.'

'Anyway, why do you need this information?' I replied, not even bothering to give him his title.

Beaufort laughed drily.

'You must know, Jankyn. Information is knowledge. Knowledge is power, and if I have it then I will use it. Will you go to France?' He saw the hesitation in my eyes. 'I admit,' he added soothingly, 'it is dangerous. Northern France is a battleground, but you will be well armed with your wits, your weapons and warrants from me, plus purses of gold and, when you return, a fortune.'

'I accept,' I hesitatingly replied, my heart thudding and my bowels almost turning to water with fright. Although I love danger, I am a born coward and I realised the perils of such a mission. 'But again I ask you. Why cannot you order such knowledge to be sent to you?'

'If I did,' Beaufort replied firmly, 'then it would alert people. So, will you go?'

I nodded my acceptance. Beaufort smiled and passed to other matters, the affairs of England and the general state of the war in France, diplomatically and deftly turning our conversation into other channels.

Later that afternoon, Beaufort with his entourage,
myself included, left the manor and took a winding path
down into the depths of the forest for a hunt. Beaufort
seemed pleased I had accepted his mission. Now,
dressed in simple brown leather and armed like a
professional hunter, he seemed to want to celebrate my
arrival as well as impress upon me his own eagerness to
taste blood. The hunt, itself, began desultorily enough.
The beaters moved amongst the thickly-twined bracken,
bellowing lustily and allowing the harts with their high
branching heads to pass without hindrance. Beaufort, a
keen expert on venery and hunting matters, had
forbidden us to harass male deer in the rutting season.
Led by the huntsmen, we entered deeper into the
forest. Beaufort pulled his horse back alongside mine to
talk quietly about my mission to France.

'Truth,' he said caustically, 'is like this hunt, Jankyn.
We go to search for something rare and brutal but
which needs to be brought to bay, and so it is with this.'
He laid a great-ringed, silver-braceletted hand on my
arm. 'If you are successful, Jankyn, I swear the manor
you have left will be yours.' He smiled. 'But if you are
not?' I think he would have said more but suddenly our
dogs scented the quarry near a thick, evil-smelling
quagmire. They gave tongue, with the chief huntsman
urging the first hounds up and spurring them on with a
splendid spate of words. The hounds, at his call, fell on
the trail they had found and streamed through the
forest howling until the trees around us echoed with
their din. Beaufort broke off his conversation and,
raising his gilt-edged horn, urged us on with its clear
treble note. We charged in a group across the forest
floor, following the hounds as they surged between
pools and spiky forest crags. At last we came to a great
rugged rock which tumbled down from a beetling cliff
to a bushy area which sheltered a marsh. We
surrounded this, aware from the barking of the hounds

that our quarry was there. The huntsmen dismounted
and beat upon the bushes with their swords, urging the
beast to come out. At last he did, swinging out with his
head slanting, seeking his tormentors. A huge, horrid,
baneful boar of unbelievable size. A solitary one long
since cut off from his herd, for he was old and cruel. He
was the biggest I have ever seen. He grunted and looked
with grim, ghastly eyes towards the dogs and then he
was through them. He hurtled three to the earth,
ripping one of them from cock to chin with his evil
yellowing tusks. Beaufort lifted his horn again and the
huntsmen took up the hallooing as we surged forward
after it. Time and again, the boar turned to tear the
dogs which attacked until these animals, fierce as they
were, became frightened of him. Our archers loosed at
him but the arrows could not pierce his flanks and
shattered on his bristling hide. Goaded and driven
demented, he dashed at the men, striking at them
savagely; he gashed one from ankle to knee and some of
the huntsmen slunk away, unwilling to continue the
pursuit. Beaufort, cool and calm as ever, urged his
horse forward to strike the beast between the eyes with
his sword but the boar rolled away, gathered its feet and
continued to flee. Eventually, we cornered it in a rocky
enclave across a small stream. Beaufort called the dogs
off and ordered his hunters to stay. He drew sword and
dagger, calmly splashing into the water to where his
enemy glared balefully at him. The beast seemed to be
aware of both the weapon and its wielder. Its bristles
stood up and, in a burst of fierce snorts, it leapt forward
eager to meet Beaufort mid-stream.

Beaufort, the water swirling around him, went down
as the beast sprang on him. I, terrified of being hurt
myself, shouted at the huntsmen to help their lord,
pretending with all my movements and arm-waving that
I, too, was doing what I could. Satan, however, looks
after his own and Beaufort was safe, sinking both sword

and dagger into the boar's heart. In a short while the thrashing and fighting stopped. Beaufort stood up smiling at us and laughing as he brushed his gleaming wet hair away from his brow while beside him the boar gently bobbed on the surface of the stream. Even in its death throes, it snarled back with teeth bare. The dogs, sensing the hunt was over, leapt into the stream to attack the dead boar and tear it to pieces. Beaufort, no longer the courtly prince or proud prelate, ordered the huntsmen to call them off. He took a huge hunting-knife from one of his companions, slashed open the boar's throat, hacking off the head and hoisting it on high to our cheers and congratulations. He dragged the boar's corpse to the bank, split the belly open and brought out the bowels to broil them on coals which one of his retainers had lit on the bank. He ripped out the entrails of the animal and threw them to the yelping, snarling dogs. After that the boar was cleansed in the stream, strung on a pole and carried back with us to the manor.

# FOUR

That night, when we had all bathed and refreshed ourselves, Beaufort held a great banquet in his hall. Tables were covered with white linen and adorned with plates, spoons, knives and the purest silver enchased with precious jewels, while his retainers served such a feast that even across the years I can remember it; sliced venison, meat broth, roasted haunch of meat, jellied soup, capons in almond milk spiced with ginger and herbs, roast pork, heron, pheasants, chicken and sweet tarts. At the end of the banquet, the great boar's head was brought in and the pastrycooks finished the meal with a four-foot high castle. This was made of pastry and topped with sponge sugar garnished with almonds and other fruits with Beaufort's arms engraved on them. I was the guest of honour, sitting at the Cardinal's right hand, whilst on my left he had placed a young lady with red hair and snow-white skin. Her face, breast and bright throat, bare to the sight, shone like a sheen of snow on the hills. This only emphasised her fiery hair and dark emerald-green gown; this was fastened with a gold girdle at the waist whilst her bright hair was covered with a net of shimmering pearls. God knows who she was. I forget her name now but she was Beaufort's gift to me. Even though I had spent a day in the saddle, I was only to willing to continue with a hunt of a different kind.

Looking back over the years, I often wonder why I

remember that hunt, the banquet and the young lady who was Beaufort's gift. Perhaps the hunt and the feasting were ways of Beaufort getting rid of his energy, as well as the hate he bore for the great nobles in London who had spurned and fought him. Ever since Henry V's death, Beaufort had grimly hung on to power, despite the threats and warnings issued by Gloucester, Henry V's younger brother. He hated Beaufort and persecuted him with savage glee. Gloucester, posing as the darling of the London mob, had even threatened to throw the Bishop and his household into the River Thames. Beaufort, so tired of this, had appealed to the Pope who, in recognition of his services, had given him a Cardinal's hat. However, that only seemed to worsen matters. Gloucester attacked him with such malicious glee that Beaufort had welcomed the opportunity to cross the narrow seas and lead a Papal crusade against the Hussite heretics in Bohemia. On his return, he had been asked to lend the Crown huge amounts of money but had received little thanks for it. Even Bedford disliked him and attempted to limit his power. So, Beaufort had returned to his manor at Cattehall and sent for me, not because he wanted the truth, but rather information to outwit his enemies, to bring them down so he could become sole Regent of England with full custody over the young and immature Henry VI. But this is all in hindsight, a virtue everyone enjoys and lays claim to, so I ask you to excuse me, for the babblings of an old, tired man who has drunk too much sack.

By the next morning, still exhausted after the previous day's hunt as well as my exertions between the sheets, I met Beaufort in the main hall. I was, the Cardinal coolly informed me, to be in France within the week and, using my wits, was to move south, cross the Loire and join the Maid's army. How I was to achieve that, Beaufort added drily, was my concern. Cynical at such help and abrupt dismissal, I packed and left immediately, securing passage on a merchant cog bound from Dover to Harfleur. The journey was dreadful. I spent three days in a tavern in Harfleur recovering from seasickness. I was determined to remove every drop of water from my clothing and baggage before proceeding along the River Seine to Paris.

This seemed to be the safest way to travel. I bypassed Rouen, for the sights on either bank were horrid to see. Rouen, itself, looked like a city which had been pillaged. The quays were empty, many houses had been burnt, and, as I passed, I saw black plumes of smoke against the sky. Those I travelled with, soldiers taking produce down to the Paris garrison, said an Armagnac force had attempted to seize part of the town, such raids into the suburbs now being common. The destruction on either side of the Seine was, as I said, horrific to behold. On many occasions as our barge stood out in mid-stream, we saw bodies floating in the shallows near the banks, children as well as men, women, horses, cattle, dogs and cats, together with the refuse and litter of war. An eerie silence hung over the countryside as if God had devastated the land wiping all the people from it. Now and again we did see riders but friend or foe we could not determine for they remained black figures against a lowering sky. Occasionally, groups of beggars, whole families, their faces white and skeletal, would come down when our barges approached the banks with their hands extended and cry piteously for alms, bread or anything to eat. Invariably, they were driven off with curses. Often, the archers who accompanied the barges would send a shower of arrows shooting through the air to drive these poor people away. The sight of the foodstuffs piled on our craft attracted even the freebooters and at a bend in the Seine they attempted a paltry ambush. They failed through poor organisation as well as the vigilance of our men-at-arms and archers.

At last, Paris came into sight. The huge towers of the cathedral of Notre Dame, the walls of the Louvre Palace, the Royal Hospital and the brick and timberwork of the grand hotels of the great lords. As it was dusk, we continued a bit further downstream, disembarking at the quay nearest the church of St. Denis. It was eerily quiet just before eight in the evening with only the church bells sounding for prayers. The area in front of St. Denis was deserted except for a few soldiers, men-at-arms all wearing English colours. I paid a visit to the dusty, deserted church, the hallowed place of Paris. It seemed to symbolise the spirit of the city, France's most holy spot, where the fourth-century martyr having been decapitated on the hill of Montmartre had actually carried his head, so legend said, down to this place of burial. His body still lies in its incorruptible state behind a glass case but, when I entered, the high altar was stripped bare with only a faint sanctuary lamp winking in its red holder. The brackets along the walls were empty of torches and the only other light came from the last rays of a weak sun piercing the stained-glass window. Benches were overthrown and huge cobwebs hung between the pillars. It was more a mausoleum than a house of God.

I left and walked through some of the narrow, winding streets. A party of soldiers wearing the Boar and Ragged Staff of the Earl of Warwick stopped and warned me that once the curfew sounded it was dangerous for anyone to be on the streets, particularly an Englishman. At every great crossroads I crossed, the niche which used to hold the statue for that particular quarter was now empty. No great bonfire or torch was lit as usual. Instead, there was scaffold after scaffold, each with its dangling corpse. Along the wide boulevards which swept through the city, huge iron chains were winched up to prevent any night attack. These prove to be an effective obstacle against enemy

cavalry. Just before darkness fell, realising my own
terrors as well as those that threatened me in the black
alleyways and rutted tracks which ran between the
narrow, tall wood and stone houses, I used Beaufort's
gold to purchase a small, dusty chamber in a tavern near
the Grand Pont.

The following morning, I bathed, changed my
clothing and taking my baggage with me decided to
wander round the capital. I had been to Paris some ten
years previously and what I immediately noticed were
the dramatic changes caused by the war. The butchers'
market near the Grand Pont was virtually empty with
very little meat on sale. I swear I saw the corpses of rats
being offered for a handful of sous. The Lombard
bankers near the Rue St. Martin had long gone. The
university on the Left Bank of the Seine seemed empty,
for few students were in the city. The grand hotels of
the Seigneurs and the Inns of Court looked as if they
had been under a siege, being badly kept, the gardens
overgrown, doors hanging off, signs faded and the
paintwork chipped and blighted. The streets were not
cleaned. The privies, cesspools, drainage pipes and
public latrines were full of refuse, dirt, offal and even
the corpses of animals. The smells in some streets were
almost unbearable. Those people who did walk carried
pomanders close against their noses to fend off the
offensive odour.

The people seemed to move in a dreamlike fashion.
There was little conversation or laughter. The
emaciated faces and staring eyes of the children were
piteous to see. The church doors were full of beggars
who were almost a multitude, an army in their own right
and everywhere were troops. Even I, an Englishman,
was taken aback by the arrogance with which they
swaggered the streets, and the horsemen, our great
captains, rode recklessly through, hawk on hand,
impervious to those who lived and worked there. The

depression in the city was like the miasma of a marsh and by late afternoon I had seen enough. I was wise and prudent enough to keep my mouth shut for the English were hated with a special virulence. I decided not to ask for any help but to travel south, trusting in my own wits to survive the horrors of France.

After buying horses in Paris, I journeyed south and crossed the Loire into the country of the Armagnacs. I now ceased to be Matthew Jankyn and changed my first name to Matthias pretending to be a Brabanter going south to offer my sword to the Dauphin. The countryside here was also devastated but, being well-armed, I suffered little trouble. The greatest plague was not the English, nor indeed the French, but the Ecorcheurs. I met one such band just after I had left Paris, their commander a dreadful young man called Richard Venables who had come to Normandy a year previously. He had massacred the inhabitants of a Cistercian monastery at Savigney and turned it into a fort from which he raided the surrounding countryside. His cruelties were unspeakable. Both French and English courts attempted to give the inhabitants some arms, even certificates of protection, but to men like Venables these proved to be nothing but worthless pieces of parchment. I am glad to say that Bedford later caught Venables and had him hanged, drawn and quartered in Paris.

The countryside both north and south of the Loire was a desert, an area of devastation. It seemed as if Satan and all his minions walked, clad in armour with great banners, committing murder and rape on a scale I had never seen or heard of before. I have spoken to travellers who had seen the effects of the Mongols in the East. I do not think it could have been any worse in north-west France in that spring of 1429. Sometimes, the crossroads seemed to be packed with a hanging crowd. In fact, they were scaffolds bearing the bodies of countless victims. Wells were infected with the corpses of animals. I would come across whole families killed, with their throats cut, their bodies decomposing as their glassy eyes stared up to Heaven. If God did not raise up someone to help the French, he should have done.

On my travels, I joined other mercenaries led by a Hainaulter, Nicholas de Couzac. He questioned me fiercely about my antecedents. I told him that I was of illegitimate birth and how I had fought at Agincourt on Henry's side but, I added with a smile, this was before the Maid appeared to lead the French. At this, the cruel bastard gave a grin. I told him that I was prepared to serve in his band and accept him as captain and he seemed to be pleased with this. One night, in a burnt-out farmhouse, one of his criminous clerks (a little, rat-faced man) drew up a crude indenture in which I promised to serve de Couzac until the end of the campaign for a certain fee and a percentage of the ransoms taken.

De Couzac and his group were a motley lot. I have seen better hanging on the Elms at Tyburn. They were landless men from different nations being Spaniards, French, Lorrainers, Germans, Saxons and even a few from the Hanseatic towns on the Baltic. There were three Scots whose accents were so atrocious that they might as well have come from Prussia. The group were all well-armed, with similar weapons to those I carried: breastplate, basinet, sword, dagger, crossbow, stout leather leggings, and feet pushed into good canvas boots. I suppose there was a form of comradeship. It certainly made my life pleasanter as I journeyed south for now I had a fresh identity with men who could not bother about my past. They were not concerned with the future and their only anxiety was the next meal and whether the next battle would be won. They were cynical men who would fight for anyone as long as the price was right, but once the money ran out so would they.

# FIVE

We had received intelligence about how the Dauphin had assembled a massive army at Blois, under the command of the Bastard of Alencon, Xantrailles, and other French captains but its real leader was Jehanne the Maid. Naturally, the mercenaries discussed this divine phenomenon. Some said she was a witch but others claimed that it was not the first time a Maid had come to help France, each with varying degrees of success. There had been Catherine who had advised the famous war captain, Guesclin, during Edward III's wars in France and, quite recently, a demented prophetess who had been burnt as a witch. Most of us accepted that Jehanne was a sorceress. Others were non-committal and a few looked scared, claiming that she could have come from God. After all, one learned man pointed out, (I think he must have been a scholar but he hid it quite successfully), there had been the prophetess, Marie, who had said that a Maid would come to deliver France from her enemies. However, such exclamations were greeted with cynical amusement if not outright laughter.

At Blois I was astonished when I saw the French camp, for the pavilions and tents spread across the fields made it look like a small city. Silken pavilions jostled with the rough, branch-entwined shelters of the common soldiers. There seemed to be chaos, although the firm hand of discipline soon became apparent. De

41

Couzac immediately offered his services, at my advice, to Xantrailles. This was refused, so we went to La Hire, one of the great mercenary captains of France. A big bastard and a fierce fighter. He took one look at our group and nodded. Indentures were drawn up in which we promised to fight in all seasons and at all times as long, of course, as the money lasted. We were then allocated places in the camp, allowed to build shelters, start fires and to picket our mounts along the horse-lines.

I was immediately desirous of catching a view of Jehanne the Maid but this was denied me so I wandered around the camp noting the different armour, pennants, flags and standards of the groups which had come there. If I had been an English commander I would have been pleased, for the army was like the Tower of Babel with contingents from all over Europe each with its own captains. It would need divine intervention to weld this force into an army. The camp was really organised chaos for not only were there foot-soldiers, cavalry and the retinues of the great nobles, but also the mercenary bands. All had flocked to the sacred Oriflamme banner to march on Orleans and deliver it from the English. Gradually, however, under the blasphemous commands issued by La Hire, order was imposed. The camp marshals enforced discipline with a strictness which I had not seen since King Henry had taken his army to Agincourt.

One morning I saw Jehanne. The news of her coming was spread by criers through the camp and we all gathered along the main avenue to watch her approach. She was dressed in white armour and was mounted on a great black destrier. I had a good view for I had pushed myself to the front. Her armour was of white silver, tempered, in the Milanese fashion, to make it lighter for the wearer. She wore an old sword bound round her waist with the blade sheathed in crimson velvet; she held a small battle-axe in one hand and in the other a huge standard. She clenched the standard firmly and on one of her fingers were the two rings, the magical symbols which the Maid always looked at even in battle. The standard was white, whether of linen or silk I don't know. It bore the Trinity with two angels in adoration on either side, with the whole field and background decorated with golden lilies. On the reverse side was a shield supported by two more angels. This bore a white dove from whose beak hung a scroll on which was written 'De Part De Le Roi Du Ciel' – 'On behalf of the King of Heaven'. As the Maid passed by, her horse picking its way gently down the rutted, muddy track, the troops on either side fell silent. Some just stared and some whispered to each other. A few, who had brought candles, took tinder, struck it and lit them, kneeling in the mud as she passed.

I just stood and gazed at her. She was small of height with a brown, weather-beaten face and dark hair cut like a page-boy around her ears. Her mouth was thin and the eyes were heavy-lidded and well spaced. Really a peasant's face, strong and stubborn. I was quite surprised. She was not the girl the King of Heaven would have chosen to lead France's armies but, then again, having seen God's method of selecting popes and bishops one does wonder what goes wrong. I later learnt that the standard had been devised at Jehanne's own bidding with her insisting on the angels. One of them, Michael, often spoke to her whilst appearing in bodily form. The sword she had obtained from the church of St. Catherine de Fierbois and maintained that God had given it to her to carry into battle. The messengers who were sent there found it resting behind the altar and brought it back. I suspect there was no act of prophesy on Jehanne's part; she must have simply known about a sword pledged to God by some Crusader in thanksgiving for a safe return from the Holy Land. The rings had been given by members of Charles' court who wished her well. I remember those rings for Beaufort would later examine them carefully and the Cardinal's interest always fascinated me.

In the main, the troops around me treated her not with disdain but fear, cautious, like animals not too sure of the mood of their master. This all sprang from one incident when Jehanne had been taken down from her native village to see King Charles. She had crossed into a castle and one of the guards had shouted out:

'Here comes the Maid. If I could spend one night with her, she would not be a maid any longer.'

Whereupon Jehanne had stopped riding, turned to the man and prophesied how, because he did not fear God, he would die unshriven by drowning. A few days later, this prophesy came true. Soldiers are superstitious creatures. They only fight on certain days. They don't like certain practices and one of them is being led by a woman who knows too much.

Nevertheless, at that first meeting I did find it hard to believe that this was France's champion against the likes of Glasdale, Falstaff, Talbot and Suffolk, who were all merry bastards who could sack a town without turning a hair on their head. She seemed to have a presence but whether this sprang from the imagination of the onlookers or because she really believed in her own mission I do not know. My first impression was that here was someone who did not dabble in black magic, witchcraft, sorcery or talking to demons. I had met that type before. Oldcastle had laid claim to such powers and such men and women always have an aura about them, something stinking or rotten. I did not pick this up from Jehanne. Now you may wonder why I, an old reprobate now past my ninetieth year, can meditate upon saints or people from God? It is simply, as I have said many times before, that the one virtue of being a rogue is how you can always detect another, even across a crowded camp.

Anyway, I digress. On that particular morning, Jehanne stopped suddenly. The cavalcade behind her, squires, friends and members of her retinue all fanned out around her. Jehanne, looking to either side, lifted herself up in the stirrups and shouted I forget the exact words but they were something like this:

'Soldiers of France! The Lord God, King of Heaven, has directed us to march on Orleans and deliver it from the hands of the Goddamns. It is God's work and we must prepare for it. Every man must be shriven, take the sacrament, and all camp followers, whores and women who are not your proper wives in the eyes of the Church, must leave the camp!'

The first part of this short speech was greeted with silence and the second with moans. There are two things a soldier hates to lose, apart from his life. The first is money and the second is his doxy. Nevertheless, in the main they obeyed Jehanne for they were too frightened of her. Indeed, the gossip was how on one occasion Jehanne had, with the flat of her sword, driven out a group of prostitutes from the camp. She claimed they had nothing to do with God's own army.

I could not really believe in Jehanne's sway over the men she led. They were the biggest group of bastards, cut-throats, pillagers and rapists I have ever had the privilege of serving with. Nevertheless, her presence caused changes. Half the army never really believed that Christ had become so concerned in the doings of France as to raise up a leader, but Jehanne's authority and her simple words seemed to achieve the desired effect. I carefully examined those closest to her, namely her brother, who was easily recognisable by the similarity in features, and one other young man whom I selected as my prey. His name, so I gathered from those around me, was Jean Delon and he was the Maid's personal squire. He looked pleased and full of pride in his position and a man full of pride can easily be tempted.

That night, I left my companions sitting with their cloaks wrapped about them, their only defence against the faint drizzle which fell as they sat in the mud playing dice and cursing quietly as the wineskin was passed around. I took my own full bottle and made my way through the muddy fields to Jehanne's quarters, a small, grey stone cottage in the fields outside Blois. Really a peasant's home and perhaps she had chosen it because it reminded her of her own origins. Set well apart from the other commanders for, quite rightly, she did not trust any of them, especially at night.

I joined a group and watched the door of the house. When I glimpsed Delon, I got up and walked towards him. I introduced myself, flattering him and his mistress. I explained how I had seen the Maid for the first time that morning, though I had heard of her exploits and the way she believed in her divine mission. The young man, a pretty young thing, seemed flattered by the attention of a veteran soldier, a professional fighter, giving grudging praise to someone who had not yet drawn sword in battle. I filled one of my two cups to the brim with rich, red Burgundy, saying it was the least I could do for one of Jehanne's retinue. He nodded his pretty blond head and as he drank I asked a favour.

'Would it be possible for me to meet the Maid?'

We were squatting under the leather awning which had been put up over the front door. Delon at first refused but I begged him, saying that I had come through northern France for this moment. He seemed satisfied and went inside. I heard low voices. Delon then came back to the door and beckoned at me.

I entered the cottage, actually no more gracious a place than the stable at Bethlehem with its mud walls and earth-packed floor. A black pot hung over a small fire in the hearth, and there was a table, rough-hewn stools and, in the far corner, a trestle-bed with a mattress of straw. The Maid was sitting there in the black clothing of a boy, with a simple jerkin and leggings. Her feet were bare. She was resting on the edge of the trestle-bed, between her hands a cup of watered wine in which she was dipping pieces of bread. She was eating slowly and staring at the floor as if concerned with some problem. When I came in, she looked up and smiled briefly. I was immediately struck as to how ordinary her face was and yet, at the same time, she had a presence. It is a kind of spiritual perfume which comes out towards the observer and you realise that you are in the presence of greatness. Whether it is divine or diabolic is another matter. Her voice was low, almost guttural, and very different to the strident voice which had declaimed to the camp that morning. She told Delon to pull a stool across for me, saying that I must not stay too long as she was tired and exhausted and would have to sleep. She asked my name and I gave it. She then asked me to describe my life, and all the time she looked at me with those chilling grey eyes, a faint smile around her lips as if she knew some joke she would not share with me. Perhaps she saw through me and knew me to be what I was. At one time, she put her cup on the ground and gently tapped me on the hand so that I could feel her calloused peasant skin.

'Matthew,' she said, 'before the battle you must get yourself shriven and take the sacrament for it is bloody work we shall be doing.'

She looked up at Delon as a sign that the interview was over so I got up and left the cottage. Only when I was outside, standing in the mud under darkened skies, did I shiver with fear. I realised that throughout the entire interview Jehanne had insisted on calling me by my English name of Matthew.

# SIX

Three days later, on the 29th April 1429, the French army left Blois for the relief of Orleans. The Maid let it be known that God, at the request of St. Louis and Charlemagne, was taking pity on the town of Orleans. He was unwilling that the English should have both the person of the Duke of Orleans, who was still held captive in England since the battle of Agincourt, and the town. Besides these two celestial beings, Jehanne was guided by two men. They were military advisers, the first of whom I have already mentioned. He was La Hire. His real name was Etienne de Vignol. He was a Gascon who had been in the Dauphin's service for almost eleven years and he was the most feared of Charles' captains. I have heard him described as being the worst, the most tyrannical and the most pitiless. La Hire was a nickname. Some people claimed that it came from the Latin 'Ira', meaning anger, while others said it came from the name of the implement used for ramming down paving-stones. Personally, I think it was the latter, having watched the fellow at close quarters. In 1421, La Hire had been injured by the fall of a chimney-piece and his consequent lameness gave him a stumping walk which easily explained the nickname as well as his scorching anger. Nevertheless, he was a brilliant soldier and horseman, even though he was a bastard. A striking figure, he had a taste for extravagant clothes, the most notorious item of which was a scarlet

49

and gold robe covered with little bells which tinkled at his every movement. His blasphemies were famous. The only person who could restrain him was Jehanne who actually persuaded him to confess his sins. One of his prayers was the most popular joke in the camp: 'God, I pray you, that today you will do for La Hire as much as you would wish La Hire to do for you if he were God and you were La Hire.'

He spoke equally frankly to everyone else, even the King.

'Sir,' he remarked on one occasion, 'I never saw a prince who more gaily lost what was his, than you.'

The other captain was Giles de Rais. At that time he was a handsome, auburn-haired man of tremendous wealth and influence, being the personal favourite of the King's chief minister, La Tremoille. Later on, of course, de Rais became notorious. I heard the stories after my return to England of how he had tortured and imprisoned hundreds of children in his castle in Brittany, practising satanic rites on them. He, too, suffered a terrible death, being burnt at the stake as an openly avowed satanist. Under these three extra-ordinary figures, our army left for Orleans.

The priests went ahead intoning the 'Veni Creator Spiritus'. Behind them came long columns of horsemen, men-at-arms, wagons – of which there were over six hundred – and four hundred head of cattle. This massive convoy of about four to five thousand men slowly lumbered along the thirty-five miles separating Blois from Orleans, bypassing Beaugency and Meung which were still held by the English. An exhausting march! We slept and rested in muddy fields and during the day had to suffer the constant discomfort of rainstorms. Nominally, I was under the command of de Couzac but whenever possible I sidled alongside Delon, the Maid's squire. At first, he looked strangely at me. I asked him why but he just muttered that after I had left,

Jehanne had remarked how we would meet again some time in the future in circumstances she would not wish. I replied that probably both of us would suffer setbacks. This seemed to satisfy the foolish young man and he chatted gaily about what was happening among the great ones who led our army. Orleans mattered to Charles and his counsellors. It lay within striking distance of Paris and, if the English captured it, the war would be lost. Charles, shambling around in his palaces, would either flee to Scotland or Spain for sanctuary and leave France to Henry VI. The siege had begun the previous October under the Earl of Salisbury who, shortly after arrival, had been killed by a cannonball. The command of the English army had now fallen into the hands of de la Pole, the Duke of Suffolk. The Burgundians, too, had joined their English allies but, when their commander had been refused certain privileges, Burgundy, in a public sulk, withdrew his forces, leaving the English to bring the city to its knees.

The French were more or less closed up in the town, which was well defended by walls reinforced at intervals by strong towers and pierced by four gates, the Port de Bourgogne, the Port de Paris, the Port Barrière and the Port Reynard. The city was also protected by a river on the south spanned by a single bridge which was commanded by two English positions, one at the Bastille de Augustines, which was a derelict church which the English had fortified, and the other a fort on the bridge known as Les Tourelles. The English had not encircled the entire city with their ring of steel. This would have been impossible, for their army was no more than six or seven thousand. Instead, they had built fortifications or bastilles. From these, they could command all approaches to the city as well as launch attacks and use their cannon to bombard the city walls.

The siege had been a desultory one. Sometimes there had been fierce hand-to-hand combat, but the main fighting was the exchange of cannon fire. One of the French culverins was commanded by a man called Maître Jean. A wag, he had a hiding-place for himself and his weapon inside the pillars of a bridge across the Loire. He was in the habit of shooting his projectiles with great accuracy to the great detriment of the English. Every now and again, in order to make fun of the English who were watching him with apprehension from their towers of fortifications, he would emerge out into the open and throw himself down on the ground pretending to be dead or wounded. Listening to the cries of self-congratulation from the English, he would get himself carried back into the city on some makeshift stretcher, only to return later to the culverin in order to teach the English that he was alive and capable of wreaking terrible damage. Of course, the great Lords still observed the mutual courtesies. On the previous Christmas, the French and English agreed to a temporary truce. Suffolk sent the French a troop of musicians while the Bastard of Orleans, the commander of the city, courteously responded by sending a warm fur coat to the Earl of Suffolk who replied with a silver dish of figs. Nevertheless, such gentle courtesies did not ignore how the siege of Orleans might determine the entire war in France. Jehanne herself realised this. Her army reached Orleans within two days at her insistence. However, there were problems, Delon explaining to me why the Maid was in a terrible rage of temper. Apparently, the famous voices who gave her commands from God had directed the line of march into Orleans should be on the north side of the river. La Hire and the other commanders insisted that it should be to the south. The commanders had taken the army by the southern route, via the village of Sologne, rather than cross the river by boats where they might be exposed to enemy attack.

When the Maid found the river Loire was between

her and Orleans, she was furious. Her anger grew when the commanders said they would ferry the provisions they had brought across to Orleans before returning to Blois for fresh sustenance. The Maid tongue-lashed her commanders, only being placated when the Bastard of Orleans (Dunois) came across with two hundred lancers to meet her. He, too, was the object of a rather spiteful lecture. The Maid declared how he should obey her God-given counsels rather than those of commanders reluctant to fight the English. The Bastard stubbornly insisted they would cross the river five miles upstream from Orleans, disembark at a village called Chesney, and so enter the city by the easiest route, the Port de Bourgogne. At the same time (and I could hear the terrifying noise) the townspeople of Orleans had attacked one of the English bastions on the Isle de Loupe. Jehanne immediately cried out:

'In God's name, the counsel of Our Lord is wiser and better than yours. You thought to deceive me but you have deceived yourselves for I bring you the finest help that was ever brought to knight or to city, since it is help from the King of Heaven.'

I heard this undignified row on the muddy banks of the Loire. Somehow or other I managed to extricate myself from my own company and get as near as possible to the Maid. Already, I had decided that if I was to accomplish my mission I would have to stay with her and was most reluctant to join the army in its retreat back to Blois. I had seen de Couzac, smoothly arguing how it would be wiser if I stayed with the Maid to keep an eye on what was going on. Of course, any plunder or ransoms I took would be shared with the rest. De Couzac looked at me strangely, murmuring something about the influence of the witch, but let me go. I then went to Delon and he agreed that I could join himself, the Maid, her two brothers, the Bastard and his two hundred lancers when they crossed the river.

'However,' he pointed out drily, 'I doubt if any of us will cross. The wind is against us and the barges cannot be taken across the river.'

'What then?' I asked.

'We will stay here,' Delon replied. 'We will be exposed to English counter-attack and that will be the end of us and the Maid's mission.'

I thought of changing my mind. Perhaps Blois was more comfortable, but there again I had no reason to believe that going back there would be any safer. Moreover, if God was protecting the Maid, he might extend a little of that protection towards me.

So I went ahead with my plan, as did Jehanne with hers, for in the middle of her argument with the Bastard of Orleans the wind suddenly changed. The barges were brought, the cattle put on board, and the Maid embarked with her entourage. Like myself, the Bastard was greatly impressed with this sudden change of weather. He begged Jehanne to leave immediately but the Maid's obstinacy continued. Finally, she persuaded the Bastard of Orleans to meet the other captains who promised that they would return to Orleans from Blois as soon as possible. Only then did we sail. I virtually threw myself aboard, happy to be away from those wet, dingy banks and heading towards what I considered to be relative safety.

We disembarked at Chesney. Jehanne stayed in a cottage of the local Seigneur while I and the others slept in his outlying barns and outbuildings. The following morning, the Maid entered Orleans, and so did I. Before I mounted, I put on my left hand a purple, gold-embossed wristguard which Beaufort had given me. Other spies in Orleans, whoever they were, would see this as a sign and arrange a meeting. We entered the centre of the town later the same day with the Maid in full armour on a white horse and Delon carrying her standard before her. I, like some clever spider, managed to insinuate myself into his affections and rode alongside him. The Maid rode at the Bastard's right hand and we were followed by many knights, squires, captains and soldiers, all in armour, and a huge crowd of citizens bringing up the rear. Other soldiers and citizens left the walls and came to meet us, men and women carrying a great number of torches so that the blackness was lit by a circle of flame and light. At their rejoicing, you would think the siege had already been raised and God, himself, had come to rescue them. The press around us was so great that a torch set fire to the pennant Jehanne carried, but the Maid struck spurs to her horse and turning it with great skill extinguished the flame. I watched this carefully, thinking that for a common peasant girl she was a born rider. Indeed, no mean feat even for an accomplished rider in full armour to make a horse cavort and yet still control it in the presence of fire.

Her act drew the shouts and cheers of the crowd who followed her religiously from the Port de Bourgogne west right across the city to the Port Reynard where lodgings had been arranged for her in the house of Jacques Boucher, the treasurer to the Duke of Orleans. By now I was considered to be an irregular member of her household so I followed her into the main hall or solar, a comfortable place with wooden panelled walls covered in blue and gold drapes. There, Delon disarmed Jehanne. Boucher indicated, with a flourish of hands, that a meal had been prepared on the table on the dais at the end of the hall. Jehanne shook her head and asked for a little wine and water to be brought. She mixed the water and wine in a silver cup and fed herself with five or six sops of bread, similar to the meal I had seen her eat a few days beforehand. We were then dismissed; Delon slept outside his mistress' chamber and I lay on the straw-covered hall floor with my cloak wrapped round me. I slept like an innocent child.

The next morning I woke up to find the hall cold and deserted. I rose and picked at some of the food left on the high table and drank a cup of full red wine to heat my body. None of the braziers in the hall were lit and I walked up and down with my hands wrapped beneath my cloak to get some warmth. I was still pacing up and down when I heard quiet footsteps and the Maid came in by a side door dressed in her usual black garb of blouse, trousers and soft boots. Her face looked white and her eyes were larger than usual. She must have had a difficult night. She rubbed her tired face in her hands and glanced sharply at me.

'Matthias!' she called out. This time, she used my pseudonym. 'Matthias, what are you doing here? You are one of de Couzac's men?'

'Madame,' I replied, 'I am with your squire, Delon, now. I asked to come and serve with you.'

Jehanne walked slowly towards me. I felt the hair on the back of my neck prickle and a cold feeling, which had nothing to do with the weather, ran up and down my spine. Like the hand of a corpse gently stroking my back. The Maid came so close I could smell a faint perfume from her. She looked steadily at me with her wide-spaced, grey eyes, quite tired but slightly amused.

'Matthew,' she said softly, 'you are a good man and yet a bad one. I detect some danger around you. What are you really doing here?'

I remember biting my lip nervously and fingering the wristguard beneath my cloak.

'I am here, like you are, Madame,' I replied, 'to do my master's bidding.'

The Maid nodded and her eyes slid away as if she had seen some of the truth but did not want to enquire into it.

'Some of my household,' she said softly, 'have gone back with the army to Blois.' She put a hand on my shoulder. 'You can stay with us. Tell Delon to rise, have some breakfast, and to join me in the chamber above.'

# SEVEN

It was Sunday, so first the Maid had to hear Mass, be shriven and receive the sacrament before she and the other captains met in the great solar of the house, a large, spacious room covered with tapestries, containing great carved oak cupboards around the walls. Some of these were open showing the treasure and wealth of their owner in a display of silver-chased cups, goblets, plate and candelabra. On the floor, there was no straw but thick Persian and Turkish carpets. Down the middle of the room ran a long, polished oak table with benches on either side of it and a great chair at each end. The Maid immediately sat on one of these chairs as if taking the position of pre-eminence before the other captains arrived.

Eventually, they did: the Bastard of Orleans conspicuous with his blond hair and long, white face; Dilieres, who was of Italian extraction, dark and swarthy, with his face a criss-cross of scar marks and one eye permanently closed; La Hire, red-haired, red-faced, limping, shouting out and cursing with every second word some foul epithet. He promptly stopped this as soon as he entered the room and saw the Maid sitting there waiting for him.

There were others. I remember one called the Sieur de Camache. He came into the room, glared at Jehanne and slumped on one of the benches, while the Bastard of Orleans sat on the chair at the far end of the table facing the Maid. At first a discussion began about what was going to happen. Delon, myself, and other members of the captains' households either leaned or crouched against the walls listening intently to what was happening and only moving when someone clicked their fingers or indicated with their hand that they wanted a goblet of wine, water or a plate of sweetmeats. Once again the Maid did not eat or drink and I wondered how she sustained herself. Was it by God's grace or Satan's magic? She seemed as impervious to hunger or thirst as she was reluctant for anyone to approach or even touch her. I had already learnt from Delon, crouched beside me wrapped in his cloak, that the previous evening she had slept with the Treasurer's wife whilst he stood guard in an adjoining room.

Discussion immediately centred around the Bastard's decision to go back to Blois to ensure the relieving army returned to help the city. The Maid loudly objected to this, saying that if he went, only herself and La Hire would be left in charge which might expose the city to an all-out attack. Moreover, if the Bastard went, he put himself at risk of capture by the English, but the Bastard continued to insist that he must go and the discussion became heated. At this point, the Sieur de Camache, who had sat glowering at the Maid with his fingers drumming on the table, suddenly spoke. Turning his back on the Maid, he addressed the Bastard.

'Why do you pay no heed,' he said, 'to our advice, but listen to that of a little sauce-box of low birth rather than to knights such as myself? I cannot see why we have to listen to such a hussy. I will lower my banner and be no more than a simple squire. I prefer to have an old man, any man here, as my master rather than serve alongside a mere girl who may once have been God knows what!'

At that, La Hire jumped to his feet shouting filthy curses, his hand going straight to the hilt of his sword, but the Bastard intervened, saying that they were there to fight the English and not themselves. Eventually, his tact, quiet speech and tone mollified both La Hire and even Camache who was persuaded to rise, go down the table and kiss the Maid on each cheek as a sign of friendship and reconciliation.

After this, the Maid accepted the Bastard's decision to leave the city on the following day. He was to return with the relief forces as quickly as possible. On his part, the Bastard agreed with Jehanne's request to send two heralds to the English with a final order from the Maid that they leave and go back to their own country. The Bastard, La Hire and the other captains could not really see the point of such a message. As La Hire said, did the Maid really think that once Suffolk and the others heard her request, they would immediately go home like children taking orders from their mother? Nevertheless, the Maid was insistent.

'We have to,' she exclaimed, 'avoid the great damage which would be brought upon the English in battle. The good Lord does not want the death of the English, especially when they are unshriven, but only that they should leave France and go back to their own country.' So the captains gave in and two heralds, Ambleville and Guienne, took the letter and left around noon.

Within an hour, Ambleville was back, his horse gone, his person covered with all sorts of filth and muck, his blue and gold tabard ripped and smeared with animal dung and even human faeces, his hose ripped, his letter torn up and his hands bound like some common felon. He had been forced to walk to our own position. He came before the Maid and the other captains and through swollen lips repeated the message the English had given him. Guienne, the other herald, they had detained, thrown into irons, and had actually prepared a stake to burn him.

The herald of a witch, so they said, did not deserve the usual courtesies of war. The English also sent other insulting news as to how the Maid was an Armagnac whore, the cowgirl of the King of Bourges. She should leave them alone and go home to mind her cows. I was in the chamber with Delon when the messenger arrived and the Maid's rage was something to behold. She went white with shock and stood quivering, trembling with rage. Her lips moved wordlessly. She glared at the poor herald as if he was responsible for the insults he brought. Eventually, Jehanne called for some wine and clutching the cup to her lips drank one or two gulps before throwing it on the floor and stalking out.

That evening, Delon and I accompanied the Maid down to the bridge which spanned the Loire. At the far end was the great tower fortress of Les Tourelles held by the English, the nearest they had got to the city of Orleans. The bridge had been destroyed in the middle but the French had built a bulwark near the end of the broken span with a huge cross above it. It was called the Belle Croix bulwark and was the closest the French could get to their opponents whilst still remaining within the safety of their own fortifications. Jehanne, dressed simply, her standard carried before her by her page, Louis de Coutes, went into the Belle Croix bulwark. A number of times, Jehanne called out:

'Glasdale! Glasdale!'

We knew Sir William Glasdale was the commander of the English forces in Les Tourelles. She received no reply. So the Maid shouted again saying that she was God's messenger and she was requesting the English, in His name, to retire or otherwise she would drive them away. No sooner had she finished than the English shouted back a roar of abuse which rose like a chorus from the great stone edifice before us. They called her 'cowgirl', saying that if they caught her she would no longer remain a maid and then they would certainly burn her. Sir William Glasdale, his figure just barely discernible on the crenellated wall, eventually bellowed that he would never surrender to a woman nor to the unbelieving pimps who followed the Maid. Jehanne, whose temper was never the most placid, became furious, white-faced and drawn, as she had been the previous morning.

'Glasdale! Glasdale!' she shouted back. 'Surrender! Surrender!'

'Oh, go away, cowgirl!' The reply was quick and sharp and even from where I stood I could hear the southern burr in his voice.

'Glasdale,' the Maid almost screamed. 'You will die, and die by drowning, without being shriven!'

The Maid's words seemed to hang in the air like a clap of thunder. The English fell silent. The Maid glared at us, left the bulwark, and stalked back across the bridge into the city.

The following three days were relatively quiet. On Sunday, the Bastard left Orleans for Blois and the city fell quiet. The Maid kept to herself but now and again went out to inspect the English positions. These were complicated and it is very difficult to give you any description as my memory, like any old man's, is beginning to fade. Basically, the English, the bastards, had ringed the city with fortifications. The main one was to the south of the city, Les Tourelles, which commanded the main bridge across the River Loire. The others were bastilles, some nine in number, with most of them on the western side of Orleans. The Maid, once more, attempted to persuade the English to go home but gave up when a fresh stream of abuse was directed her way. I accompanied her, and she seemed to accept me into her retinue without any further demur, albeit, on one or two occasions, I caught her slyly looking at me as if trying to decide who I really was. Delon had gone with the Bastard to Blois, so there were occasions when I had actually to serve the Maid either with a cup of watered wine or by polishing her armour or tending to her horse. I was not concerned. My knowledge of French was fluent enough. Only Beaufort and I knew that I was a traitor. My main concern was twofold. First, that I would not be killed in some ugly mêlée around the city, and second, that I would not be captured by the English who might execute me as a traitor or turncoat. I did feel uncomfortable in the Maid's presence. I had achieved my end in speaking to and getting close to her, but I could see that she did not trust me and perhaps did not like me. Nevertheless, I felt an unease, a tension, whenever she was physically near me, so I decided to find quarters elsewhere.

The Maid's arrival in Orleans had created a stir. The excitement amongst the civilian population was intense, like flames leaping amongst the stubble. Anyone who had come with the Maid was treated with the same respect and veneration. After wandering around the wine-shops and market-places, I eventually struck up an acquaintance with a young widow whose husband had been killed in the previous fighting. She had a comfortable two-storey house near the Port Barriére. I used all my considerable skill, diplomacy and tact to secure lodgings with her in a clean, small garret under the loft. The floor was swept and covered with herbs. There was a battered chest, stool and small table, and a feather-down mattress thrown on the floor in the corner with a blanket. I paid the woman well both for the room and for some hot food. The latter tended to be a mixed mess of vegetables served up from the great pot which hung over the fire in the small hall of the house.

She was a comfortable little woman, small, brown-skinned, with bright shining eyes. She treated me as a hero, which was a role often assigned to me and one I never deny. Of course, I received other comforts. One night when she joined me in my room we had the merriest time on my mattress, her pleasant ministrations being a welcome relief to the tensions I had felt during the day. I had one other worry. I constantly wore the purple wristguard Beaufort had given me, but so far no one had attempted to approach me. I wondered if Beaufort's scheme was simply some madcap plot which would fail to reach fruition.

My own concerns were overcome by a surge of events in Orleans. On Tuesday, 3rd May, soldiers from surrounding garrisons such as Chateau Reynard came into Orleans, many on foot. They entered the Port de Bourgogne late in the evening with the news that the army from Blois was on its way. Immediately, mounted guards were posted day and night in the belfries of the churches of St. Pierre and St. Paul. On the following day, with the tocsin booming out, a breathless guard rushed into the courtyard of Boucher's house, yelling that the relief army was on its way. The Maid ordered five hundred lancers to accompany her and, unfortunately, I was one of them. I am not the best of horsemen, so I despaired of myself as we left the town at breakneck speed in hot pursuit of the Maid's fluttering banner which, in my terror, I thought signalled our journey to every English soldier in the besieging force. Perhaps God was on our side; we trailed across the open spaces, undefended by walls, trenches or fortifications, but not one English soldier came out against us. No arrow was loosed or bombarde fired. Eventually our small force met the Bastard's army and, unscathed, we returned in triumph back into the city.

I still remember entering Orleans on that late spring morning with the fresh troops and supplies. The excitement was infectious. I made a decision, born out of sheer boredom, to wait and see how matters turned out. Perhaps even join the French and take heavy ransoms to acquire gold and wealth. The future seemed rosy. So far, I had been in France for weeks and had not once been attacked. Perhaps it was an augury for the future. I wished to God that I had dismissed such

illusions immediately and clambered over the fortifications to run screaming into Suffolk's arms. I should
have listened to my common sense and spared myself
many a hard knock and terrifying moment.

The rest of the day the Maid rested, and I spent most
of it in Boucher's house chatting to Delon. It was about
midday when a messenger came in, followed by the
Bastard of Orleans, bearing news that Sir John Falstaff
was bringing fresh reinforcements for the English
besiegers. The Maid immediately reasserted herself
and, dressed in half-armour, she shouted across the
room.

'Bastard, Bastard, in God's name I order you to let me
know as soon as you hear of Falstaff's coming. If he
passes without my knowledge, I promise you I will have
your head off!'

Orleans, for once in his life seemingly lost for words,
shrugged and walked away. The Maid, perhaps
overcome by the excitement of accompanying the relief
army into Orleans and the news that an impending
battle could not be many days off, declared herself tired
and went upstairs to rest.

I am not too sure about the sequence of events after
that. Everyone I have talked to has admitted they are
shrouded in a mist of confusion and speculation. The
bare facts seem to be these. The English, as I said, had
besieged the city by building a series of bastilles around
it. To the east was the Bastille de St. Loupe, which was
rather isolated as most of the English force was based
to the west of the city. Whether it was at some
commander's insistence or whether the citizens of
Orleans were overcome by excitement, I do not know.
But, late on that Tuesday afternoon, an attack was
launched against the Bastille in the hope of driving the
English out. I am not too sure how the Maid got to
know. I was dozing, which was not due to fatigue or
tiredness but to too much wine and my exertions the

previous evening. Upstairs, the Maid was asleep and Delon was also in the adjoining chamber. Delon later claimed that he had only just settled down to rest and was half-asleep when suddenly the Maid sprang from her bed and kicked him awake. He asked, in God's name, what she wanted.

'In God's name,' she replied, using her favourite oath, 'my voices have told me to go against the English, but I do not know whether it is against one of their forts or against Falstaff who is on his way with supplies.'

The Maid then became frantic and hysterical. She ran throughout the entire house yelling for her armour and sword and shouting for her horse to be brought out and saddled. So intent was she on leaving that her little page, her hostess, Boucher's wife, and Boucher's daughter, Charlotte, had to arm her. Her chaplain, Jean Pasquerel, a small, grey saintly man, came in, alarmed at the excitement. The Maid shouted at him:

'Where are they? Where are the people who are supposed to arm me? The blood of our people is red on the ground!'

Meanwhile, news of the attack on the Bastille de St. Loupe had travelled back into town. There were shouts and cries in the streets that an English counter-attack was doing great harm to the French. I met Jehanne, dressed in half-armour, as she virtually ran down the stairs. She stopped, looked at me, and grabbed me by the arm.

'Hah, sanglant garçon,' she said, 'you never told me the blood of France was being spilt. Go, get my horse!'

I took it from the stables, threw over it the saddle, harnessed it properly and led out my own beast. I hurried back into the house, took up my own breastplate, swordbelt and dagger and rushed out into the courtyard to join the Maid. The little page-boy, Louis de Coutes, was already there. The Maid immediately came out and shouted at him to go back and get her standard, which he did, passing it to her through the window. Seizing the banner in one hand, she looked around before galloping off towards the Burgundy gate with her horse travelling so fast it struck sparks from the cobbles. I mounted and followed her with Louis de Coutes running after us.

The cobbled streets were packed with people. We forced our way through the narrow, winding alleyways and past the timbered, overhanging houses into the main boulevard which led down to the Port de Bourgogne. Here, we met the first trickle of casualties, with four dust-covered men-at-arms carrying a stretcher. The man lying on it had the most horrific stomach and head wounds. The blood oozed blackly out, staining the stretcher while the man writhed in wordless agony. The Maid stopped her horse, looked down at the man and said:

'I can never see French blood without my hair standing on end.'

She spurred her horse on. I followed suit, my heart sinking with dread as I drew my sword and waved it in the air shouting 'St. Denis, St. Denis!' Other horsemen joined us and we galloped out through the gate down towards the Bastille de St. Loupe. The English were trying to succour the small garrison there of about a hundred and thirty men but this relief force was cut off by a second company of mounted French soldiers who issued from the gate and engaged them in fierce hand-to-hand combat. We could hear the noise and din of battle away to our left. We pressed on through our own stragglers and wounded to the very base of the bastille, a large earthenwork building around a derelict church. The fighting there was mainly hand-to-hand. Jehanne pushed her horse through and I followed. An English man-at-arms came at me with his steel, conical hat off, his face covered in dirt, his eyes staring and his lips drawn back in a grimace of hate. He lowered his pike and jabbed towards my leg. I moved my horse and bringing my sword down in one quick curve cut him in the neck. He fell away in a great arc of spurting blood. All around me were the beginnings of a bloodbath. A host of French, armed with lances, swords, leaden maces and battle-axes, mercilessly flayed the English until the ground underneath became slippery with blood and littered with corpses.

The French pushed the English back into the bastille. Assault-ladders were placed against the wall and soldiers scrambled up, protected by their bucket-type helmets and large pavises strapped to their backs. They looked like beetles climbing up some stalk. The shields, or pavises as they were called, had been developed by the French for attacking fortified positions. They were unlike the usual shield. It was not carried before the chest but was worn upon the back so the wearer might creep or run forward in a stooping position and be relatively safe from any shower of stones, arrows or boiling oil. The construction was simple, ordinary barrels were cut in half, covered with stout leather, reinforced with hoops, and then fitted with two leather straps nailed to the inside through which the arms were slipped. This contrivance was large enough not only to cover the buttocks and back but also the head of the wearer.

At the top of the wall, the English manned the ramparts and kept up a furious defence, pouring down stones, oil and even the deadly little caltrops, the spiked balls which would pierce a man's foot and lame him for life. Nevertheless, more scaling-ladders were placed against the wall and the French swept up, clearing the ramparts. In a short while, the main gates of the bastille were swung open and the Maid, followed by myself and other lancers, cantered into the courtyard before the derelict church. Inside, the scene was one of absolute desolation and devastation. The ground was strewn with corpses. The English had taken refuge in the belfry. Those unlucky enough not to reach there had been cut down. Some fell on their knees begging for quarter, but the French had the bloodlust upon them and throats were cut and heads lopped off without a second thought. The other French commanders wanted to direct an assault upon the church but the Maid refused.

'The door is fortified,' she shouted. 'We cannot take it, so we will starve them out!'

Hardly were the words out of her mouth when the most surprising event occurred. The doors of the church opened and about forty men came out, all dressed in priestly garb of stoles, albs and surplices. I looked closely. Priests? Monks? I suddenly realised that the English had come out to sue for terms but, fearing a massacre, had first dressed in sacred vestments to win some clemency from their victors. Next to Jehanne, La Hire pulled out his sword and held it up by the hilt.

'They are English,' he said. 'They were asked to surrender. They did not. Let them all die!'

But the Maid, taking off her helmet, stood up in her stirrups and shouted out:

'These are prisoners. They are men of the church.' I caught the irony in her voice. 'Consequently, they must be protected. They are our prisoners. Bind them and bring them back to Orleans.'

So they did, and the Bastille de St. Loupe fell into French hands.

# EIGHT

That evening, Joan wept, so Delon later told me, for the English who had died unshriven and offered up prayers that God would have mercy upon them. I was too exhausted and frightened to do anything. I could still see that English man-at-arms falling away with his blood arching against the sky. I ruefully realised it could well have been me. That night, I took my pretty young widow in a rough, ungentlemanly fashion, squeezing her flesh and making her squeal. As if by clinging on to her, I could convince myself I was still alive.

I was also concerned at what I had seen in that battle. The Maid seemed to have a presence. The attack on the bastille had been a success, partly because the French grossly outnumbered the English, but also because they seemed to be fired by an enthusiasm which I had not seen before. I wondered if Beaufort was right. Did the Maid have secret powers? So far, everything I had seen indicated she had no dealings or connivance with witches, warlocks, wizards or anything diabolic. So was I involved in the betrayal of one of God's saints? I am not a religious man but lying beside the widow I looked into the darkness and wondered what part I really should play.

The following day, Thursday, the 5th May, was Ascension Day. Because of the solemnity of the feast, the French, under the Maid's guidance, decreed there would be no fighting. The Maid added that all men were to be shriven and take the sacrament and women of ill-repute should leave the ranks of the army. I found her dictating this to a clerk in a small chamber off the main hall of the Treasurer's house. I stood there while she finished her instructions. She looked menacingly at me and I thought she was going to include my widow but her eyes fell away. She asked the clerk to re-read her instructions, nodded and then went back up to her own private chamber.

An hour later, a great Council meeting was held in the Treasurer's hall. All the leading captains were present as well as some of the chief citizens of the town. They decided a powerful feint attack should be launched on the English-held Bastille de St. Laurent, to the west of the city near the river. The real assault would be against the great English fortress of Les Tourelles. For some strange reason, Jehanne was not included in this session. When she heard about it she called Delon and myself, ran down the stairs, bursting open the chamber doors and stalked angrily around the room demanding to be told what had been decided. At first, they were reluctant. until the Maid confronted the Bastard and shouted:

'Tell me what you have really decided. For God's sake, I should know how to keep a far greater secret than that.' The Bastard replied courteously:

'Jehanne, do not become angry. We cannot tell you everything at once. We have decided there should be a feint attack against the Bastille de St. Laurent. If the English divert forces there, we shall cross the bridge and do whatever we can against them in Les Tourelles. We consider this plan good and profitable.'

The Maid stood quietly biting her lip. She nodded and stalked back to her own chamber where she called for her confessor, Father Pasquerel, to dictate a letter to him. He wrote a rough draft and then again on a small piece of parchment. I can, across the years, still remember her very clear message:

'You, men of England, who have no right to be in this kingdom of France. The King of Heaven commands you, through me, Jehanne La Pucelle, to abandon your forts and to go back where you belong, which if you fail to do I will make such a disturbance as will be eternally remembered. I am writing to you for the third and last time. I shall not write any more. Jesus, Maria. Jehanne La Pucelle.' She added a postscript: 'I would have sent you my letter in a more honourable manner but you have detained my herald called Guienne. Please send him back to me and I will send back some of your people captured at St. Loupe for they are not all dead.'

Once the final draft was written, she asked Father Pasquerel to read it out to her again and again before she pronounced herself satisfied. She rolled it, sealed it with a small blob of wax and handed it to me.

'You know how to use an arbalest, a crossbow?' I nodded, my heart sinking, for I knew what she intended. 'Then, Matthias, take this on to the bridge and fire it into the garrison of Les Tourelles. Go as far as St. Croix. You will be safe.'

I breathed a deep sigh, took the message and clattered down the stairs. The Maid came after me.

'Matthew,' she called softly. I turned and looked at her. She held my gaze with her steel-grey eyes. 'Matthew,' she repeated. 'If you wish, you can take it personally. You do understand?'

I nodded and continued down to the courtyard. I took a crossbow from the stores, went across the bridge to St. Croix and there, hoisting up a piece of white cloth, shouted:

'Read, here is news!'

I winched the bolt back which carried Jehanne's scroll and, aiming it at the battlements of Les Tourelles, let loose. The bolt whizzed through the air and there was silence for a few minutes. At last a figure appeared on the battlements.

'Ah,' the man shouted, 'so we have news from the harlot of the Armagnacs. Go, tell the cowgirl to mind her cows and to watch herself. If we catch her we shall surely burn her like we intend to burn her herald.'

I waited a few more minutes before returning to give the Maid their message. She looked at me, burst into tears and hurried off to her room.

I spent the rest of the day walking the streets. They were deserted. The shops had little to sell. The meat markets, vegetable markets and spice markets were all closed. The cobbled streets were empty for business was sparse and few people ventured abroad, frightened of the occasional bombarde or stone hurtling through the air. I had been in Orleans but never really knew the city. To me, it was a collection of winding, cobbled streets, stinking alleyways, houses crouched together with the top storey jutting out above the rest, some made of plaster, others of stone. That day, I took careful note of my surroundings for, as I walked, I became aware I was being followed. Nothing certain or definite, just the faint slither of leather on the wet cobbles behind me. I turned and saw a glimpse of a cloak being pulled back and someone sheltering in a doorway. I fingered the leather wristguard, happy at last that someone had recognised me, as the Maid's attitude was beginning to trouble me. Did she know I was a spy? Did she know I was there for her own destruction? If so, would she not denounce me. Did she hope that when I went out to the St. Croix Bastille I might be killed or captured? Was she, in a sense, telling me to go? I wondered about her and her voices. Were they fantasies, phantasms of the dark, diabolic acts or definite messages from God? I had seen deluded people before, men who had followed causes, religious or political. They had all died violent, barbaric deaths. Would the Maid be the same? I wondered if I should desert, go back to Beaufort and tell him I could learn nothing for nobody had contacted me. However,

Beaufort, cunning as a fox, would have devised some stratagem so, if I escaped, something would happen to me, either being betrayed to the French as a spy or handed over to the English as a renegade. I decided to bide my time and made my way back to my quarters and the warm, brown comfort of the little widow woman.

The following morning, for some inexplicable reason, the French plan of attack was abandoned. Instead, it was decided to send a force across the river, using a pontoon of boats, to take the small English outpost of St. Jean le Blanc. This was accomplished very quickly with the English withdrawing and falling back on the stronger and bigger Bastille des Augustins. The French, when they saw this, realised that this bastille was too great a target for them and began to retreat. At this moment, the Maid, La Hire and I arrived on the far bank. The Maid looked round, took in the situation at a glance, and, drawing her sword, charged across the pontoon bridge with La Hire in pursuit and I, rather tardily, behind. Once we had reached the place, the Maid dismounted, went into the ditch to plant her standard for all of us to follow, and was wounded in the foot by a caltrop. Yet she refused to retreat and waved the troops on.

Two of our men, Goncourt and a Spanish mercenary called Pastada, settled a dispute about who should go first by joining hands and running to the foot of the palisade. There, a powerful Englishman, well-equipped and armed with a great two-handed sword, was fiercely resisting our attack on the palisade. Luckly, Jean de la Reine, the famous culverin shooter, was also present, and, at the Maid's behest, he sighted this English warrior and shot him clean through the head. The Bastille des Augustins was then stormed in a bloody, vicious fight. We penetrated the palisade and reached the open ground beyond where a fierce hand-to-hand fight took place. Many English escaped over the far

fence and fled towards Les Tourelles. The rest were cut
down with no quarter being given. It was like a butcher's
yard. I saw legs, heads and arms all strewn about, great
pools of congealing black blood, soldiers in various
positions clutching hideous, gaping wounds and one
young English archer with a look of surprise on his face
as he tried to stuff his blue entrails back into a gaping
stomach wound.

Once the garrison was taken care of, I made sure that
I was not involved in any of the hand-to-hand fighting. I
ran round waving my sword, shouting magnificently as
if I was a hero at Roncevalles. Then the general plunder
began. There were stores, provisions, arms and a few
camp followers. These were roughly taken, bound, and,
without the Maid suspecting, smuggled out to be taken
back to the camp for the pleasure of other comrades.
The Maid, bleeding copiously from her foot, realised
the situation was getting out of hand. Her troops were
disorganised and the English might launch a counter-
attack. She ordered the bastille to be set on fire and the
French withdrew.

The Maid limped home and had the wound tended to
without much fuss, allowing wine to be poured over it so
the flesh was clean before being bandaged. She then
sat down to a light supper. Her confessor, Father
Pasquerel, persuaded her that because of the fighting
and the injury she had sustained, she must break her
usual routine of fasting. While she was eating, Delon
and myself being in the same chamber, ᵗhe Bastard sent
a message saying there was no further need for any
sorties. The Maid immediately snapped back:

'You have been with your counsel and I have been
with mine.' This was a reference to her voices. 'Believe
me, my counsel will be accomplished. Yours will come to
nothing.' She then included Pasquerel, Delon and
myself in one sweeping, hard-eyed glance. 'Get up early
tomorrow, even earlier than you did today, and do the

best you can. You must stay near me all the time for tomorrow I shall have much to do, more than I have had yet, and the blood will flow from my body just above my breast.'

I once asked Delon how her voices spoke. He said he did not know except that sometimes he found her in a trance, after which she informed him that St. Michael, St. Margaret and St. Catherine often appeared in a pool of light, which he never saw, and spoke to her. I disbelieved this as I did her gift of prophecy, but that night and the following day I had good cause to change my mind. This only deepened my sense of guilt at being involved in the Maid's betrayal.

There was great apprehension in Orleans that night. The narrow, cobbled streets were packed with citizens. Merchants in their beaver hats and thick, serge cloaks; matrons in long, flowing dresses bound at the waist by gold and with wimples on their heads; young apprentices; hard-bitten veterans; they all sensed something was going to happen. It was like a forest fire which springs up in the driest of summers with a flame here and a flame there and, suddenly, there is a conflagration. So it was in Orleans that night. There was a sense of excitement, of apprehension. People bustled around the streets bringing food and wine to the soldiers. Any man wearing armour and a sword was hailed as a hero and kissed by all and sundry. I made sure I had my fair share. I met de Couzac and others of my contingent. When I told them I was with the Maid, de Couzac looked at me strangely, muttered something about every man to his own and wandered off. He came back and said that any ransoms, of course, must be divided with the company because of the indenture I had drawn up with him. I agreed and he walked away again. The tocsin was sounded many times that night. The city guards had seen fires in the English camp. Suffolk had apparently learnt his lesson and was beginning to withdraw from and burn those bastilles and outposts which could not withstand a concerted attack. Small contingents of English, out on the isles in the middle of the river Loire, also took to their boats. Apparently in great haste and fear, for two turned over and when dawn broke we saw their steel-encased bodies bobbing, face-down, in the shallows.

On the 7th May, the Maid decided to launch an all-out attack against Les Tourelles. The day was beautiful, with sheer blue skies, a few white, fleecy clouds and the Loire sparkling under a brilliant sun. Even the town, despite the mounds of manure and offal which littered the streets and the damaged buildings hit by the great boulders from the English cannons, looked golden and fresh. It was not a day for dying or turning the river red with blood or seeing bodies piled like rags in heaps.

To understand the ensuing battle, you must understand the Tourelles. They were two huge stone towers near the head of the broken bridge across the river Loire. These towers were protected on the Orleans side by a gap in the bridge, with the gap itself being further protected by an outwork. On the other side, or southern side away from Orleans, the towers were protected by a deep ditch and palisades. Between these and the Tourelles was the river, which could only be crossed by a drawbridge. So if the palisades were rushed the English could retire into the Tourelles, raise the drawbridge and defy the enemy. There were six hundred of the best English soldiery manning these defences under one of their greatest captains, Sir William Glasdale.

The towers then were the key to Orleans. If the English advanced from them, Orleans would be theirs. If the Maid drove them off the bridge, it would give the city a clear path into the surrounding countryside and allow the Bastard of Orleans to launch flanking attacks on the English positions. Everybody knew this and discussed it as if they were a Caesar or a Pompey. Me? I spent the night squatting over the latrines, quaking with terror!

# NINE

The Maid rose early, as did Delon and myself. Jehanne heard Mass and breakfasted. A minor incident revealed her gift of prophecy and certainty in her divine mission. Jacques Boucher, the Treasurer and her host, brought a fish into the house.

'Jehanne,' he said. 'Eat this fish before you go.'

'In God's name,' the Maid replied, 'we will not eat it until supper when we have re-crossed the bridge and brought back Englishmen to eat their share.'

The Maid then left with Delon carrying her standard and I behind him. We clattered out of Boucher's courtyard and into the city. The frenetic excitement of the previous evening had not died down. As Jehanne passed through the narrow, cobbled streets, with her standard snapping in the early morning breeze, crowds began to follow her. She headed straight for the Port de Bourgogne, totally determined to launch an attack straight against the Tourelles. At the gate, a knight, de Goncourt, tried to prevent her from leaving, but the Maid was in such a temper and the crowds so determined to follow her out that he had to give way. We got through and headed south to overrun the Tourelles. We reached the bastille at around six o'clock and the Maid immediately called a council of war. We had approached the fortification from the south and the first move was to storm the earthwork which protected it. At seven, our trumpets brayed out and our

lines advanced, steel-encased figures walking across the
rubble. Every so often, we would stop and shout,
'Hurrah, St. Denis! St. Denis!'

We came to the edge of the ditch. Jehanne, once
more, planted her standard. We brought forward
scaling-ladders. The English, opposite, immediately
tumbled us down, firing on us with cannon and other
firearms and attacking with axes, lances and lead
slingshots. They even tipped scalding oil over us and I
saw men boiled alive in their armour, screaming
frantically for some solace from the terrible heat. Time
and again that morning we went back to cross the ditch
to take the earthwork. It was no chivalrous fight. The
air hung heavy with the smell of oil, burning flesh and
sulphur. We were figures in the darkness, coughing and
spluttering. In a way, I thank God for one thing. I did
not want to cross the scaling-ladder and be tumbled
down into the ditch to lie there waiting for some English
marksman to finish me off. Instead, I roamed up and
down the edge shouting and gesticulating with my
sword. I kept a sharp eye open for an Englishman
cunning enough to realise that I was a suitable target.
Then, just before recall, a cry went up and I ran along
the ditch and saw the Maid. She was attempting to put a
scaling-ladder up against the wall when a crossbow bolt
had gone into her just above the breast and pierced her
shoulder. The Maid was on her knees. Her hand
clasped the wound and through it I could see the red
blood seeping. Her white face was contorted with pain. I
scrambled down the ditch towards her but the Sieur de
Camache, who had previously sworn that he would
rather give up his banner than serve under her
command, gallantly rode up to defend her with his axe.
Some of the English were already beginning to descend
the palisade to surround her.

'Take my horse,' he said and he pushed her on. The
Maid allowed herself to be led away from the battle. I

followed and watched her pull the bolt out with her own hands. Some soldiers, resting between rallies, came up wanting to recite charms to cure her but she drove them away with curses saying it was against God. So they staunched the blood for her, dressing the wound with olive oil and lard and covering it with linen cloths.

By eight o'clock, the ground in front of the Tourelles was littered with dead, dying and wounded soldiers, yet still we had made no impression on the English. All my companions, those who had followed the Maid, which included the greatest captains like La Hire and the Bastard of Orleans, were covered in sweat. Their faces were black and they all had scratches and minor wounds. Eventually, the Bastard ordered his trumpets to sound the recall and we retreated back to our own positions. The Maid joined us. The Bastard bluntly informed her that sufficient unto the day was the evil thereof, but the Maid begged him to give her some time and she went off into a small nearby copse to pray. When she came back, I saw her in argument with the Bastard of Orleans. There seemed to be some confusion over her standard and, suddenly, a man was running forward with it flapping in the breeze, its pure whiteness still clear despite the dirt and filth of the day. The fellow seemed to have a charmed life for he reached the foot of the wall and planted it there. The whole French force gave one massive roar and surged forward in a line. The attack on the wall was bitter and even I was there, covering my head with a shield, helping others up the scaling-ladder but making sure I went up last.

At the same time, on the other side of the bridge on the Orleans side, the French had caught the excitement and exhilaration, perhaps by hearing the massive roar coming from the southern bank. They brought carpenters with ladders and gutter-pipes and throwing them across, endeavoured to span the gap in the broken bridge. Eventually they did and the English found they were being attacked on both sides. The panic spread. I later heard Englishmen claiming they saw visions in the sky. The Maid, now in command of both ditch and rampart, shouted out:

'Glasdale, Glasdale, surrender yourself! Surrender yourself to the King of Heaven! You have called me "harlot" but I have great pity on your soul and the souls of your men!'

Glasdale, the old rogue, never stopped but retreated to the drawbridge which led back into the Tourelles. Unfortunately, a large boat full of faggots, horse-bones, shoes, sulphur and all the stinking things one could find, had been run under the drawbridge which joined the Tourelles to the bank. Once in position, the barge was set on fire. The flames crackled underneath the bridge, licking at the thick-seamed wood. Meanwhile, Glasdale and thirty of his best men who had formed a rearguard as a force within the earthwork, broke and made a dash for the limited safety of the Tourelles. By the time they tried to cross the drawbridge, the fire had taken hold and the drawbridge collapsed beneath them. Glasdale was drowned, thus fulfilling Jehanne's prophecy that he would die by drowning, as did a number of others. This proved too much for the English, who threw down their arms and begged to surrender. The prisoners were taken back to Orleans. The Tourelles was set alight and it blazed like a beacon for the city to see, reddening the water of the Loire. All the bells of Orleans began to ring out, with priests and people flocking into the churches to sing the 'Te Deum Laudamus'.

Meanwhile, Jehanne had gone back to the south bank and there allowed her wound to be re-dressed whilst eating bread and drinking wine. I sat beside her as the humble hero, yet throughout that entire day I had never struck a blow. The Maid was upset that Sir

William Glasdale had died. I really think she would have liked to have had her hands on him after the names he had called her. His body was later fished up out of the river, cut into pieces, boiled and embalmed and then allowed to lie for a week in the chapel with candles burning night and day, before being sent back to England for burial.

On the night following the fall of the Tourelles, the Maid and the other French commanders rested and slept after their great victory. The next day, the English de-camped and arranged themselves in order of battle. News of this was brought to our quarters. The Maid immediately arose from her bed and, dressed only in a coat of mail because of the wound she had received, forbade any attack so that the English could retire without any pursuit. Nevertheless, La Hire and the other captains insisted they confront the English. The order was reluctantly given and, late in the morning, the French army filed out of Orleans to take up its battle position opposite the English. Two long lines of mounted knights and foot-soldiers faced each other. I was seated behind Jehanne looking across the green, mud-strewn fields and had a clear view of the English lines with the banners of their commanders very clearly clustered in the centre.

For a while, the Maid watched as the English began to withdraw, before sending for a portable altar and asking her confessor to celebrate Mass there with the whole army as the congregation. Once the Mass was over, Jehanne sent scouts out with one instruction, to see if the English were turning their faces or their backs. The scouts returned a short while later claiming that the English had turned their backs in full retreat. The Maid was pleased, saying that it was God's will they did not fight the English on a Sunday and that the French would get them another time. Some of the captains, however, overjoyed to see the enemy in retreat, did order a pursuit to capture cannons and to loot what was left of the English camp. In the process, they managed to free the poor herald, Guienne, who had been left chained to a post.

Over the next few days, the Maid, though criticised for allowing the English to withdraw, composed herself and left, with a small retinue, for Tours and Loches to meet the Dauphin whom she now wished to crown King. I remember the time well; the bright summer days, white palaces, beautiful samite hangings, gold cups, haughty officials in blue and gold tabards, trumpets braying and perfumed ladies with their noses high in the air. Finally, of course, Georges La Tremoille, the King's chief minister. An obese man, with eyes like blackcurrants in a white, oily, puffy face which, according to rumour, masked a sharp, keen brain. He was Beaufort's rival at every turn. Indeed, a man who could look after his own, being as cunning and artful as any fox. Then there was Charles himself. Poor, knock-kneed, dribble-mouthed Charles.

I wondered what God saw in him, let alone the Maid. She called him 'Gentle Prince', 'Dauphin', or even 'Oriflamme', but when I saw him he was nothing much. His limbs were thin and frail. God, it was shocking to see him walk about without his great cloak on and dressed in his usual short tunic of green cloth with matching hose which only made him look ridiculous. He was very ugly with small, grey, wandering eyes and his nose was thick and bulbous. He also had a reputation for piety and self-indulgence but was very envious of people more definite and successful than himself.

When I saw him greet the Maid, he refused to allow her to kneel in his presence. Despite the honour he showed her, I knew that if I had been the Maid I would not trust such a prince as far as I could spit. Once I mentioned this to Delon but the squire was hot in Charles' defence: the Dauphin's mother was to blame,

she had been a harlot who had openly declared her son
might be illegitimate and was constantly ridiculing him
with this fact. His father had a streak of insanity which
sometimes reduced him to a quivering mass, frightened
of everything such as crossing bridges or even sitting
down. Sometimes he was so mad he claimed he was
made of glass and would not allow anyone to touch him
in case he shattered.

Jehanne spent most of her time either at Tours or
Loches going on her knees and putting her arms round
the Dauphin's thin, spindly legs, begging him to
accompany her to Rheims to receive the sacred oil and
be declared King of France. I soon found out, however,
with my nose for mischief, that the Dauphin was
frightened. He was frightened of his own shadow, of
the English, of the Maid and, above all, big Georges La
Tremoille, who counselled caution by pointing out how
the English armies were still roaming France and the
Dauphin could be captured. In despair, the Maid
returned to Orleans, Delon and I with her. She spent
two weeks there receiving the plaudits of the crowd as
well as presents of red and green cloaks from the
Bastard of Orleans, together with a beautiful white and
gold surcoat which she wore over her armour. The
Maid may have been a saint but she was still a woman
conscious of her appearance, desperately anxious to be
accepted by everyone.

I returned to my jolly little widow and whiled away
the time teaching her new skills in bed whilst keeping
one sharp ear tuned to what might be happening. I still
wore the purple wristguard but was now oblivious to
any agent Beaufort might send to Orleans. I should
have been on my guard. I knew Beaufort well and the
strings were pulled when I least suspected it. One night,
I was walking up a dark, dank alley. It was a poor area
of the city with narrow, wooden hovels crowded against
each other and the upper chambers blocking out the sky

above. I felt safe enough with my sword strapped round me, my hand on the hilt like a hero from the war coming home after a night's carousing. Suddenly, a cloak was thrown over my head, my arms were pinioned behind me and I was pulled into one of the houses. I could smell stale sweat, urine, boiled cabbage and rotting food. I know them well. They are the odours of poverty and deprivation.

'Who are you?' I spluttered. I already had a faint idea, for if they had just been thieves my throat would have been cut. I cursed myself for being caught off guard because I was usually cautious about my own safety. Yet the protection of Jehanne and the victory of Orleans had convinced me that I was some form of veteran, professional soldier who was capable of looking after himself.

'Who are you?' I repeated. My assailants did not answer. I was pushed down on a stool. The cloak, with a slight gash in it for me to breathe, was still over my head. Then I heard a faint snigger. My blood ran cold and I felt a shiver of ice go up my back for I knew whoever was there was truly evil. Beneath the rottenness of that small house, there was a spiritual dirt. I was in a malignant presence and sensed it. I could not tell whether there were two or more. I sat and waited.

'You are Jankyn, Matthew Jankyn?' The voice was cold and incisive. I did not reply. I felt the prick of a sword or dagger against my bare throat. 'I asked you a question,' the man said. 'You are Matthew Jankyn?'

'Yes,' I said wearily, 'I am Matthew Jankyn and I am wearing a purple armguard on my wrist.'

'It is a well-known sign of penance, and Beaufort sent you?' Again there was the low snigger and I realised the laughter in the darkness came from someone else and not the speaker. 'You are with the Maid, La Pucelle, the Armagnac whore?' the voice repeated.

'For the while, I am serving in the Dauphin's army,' I replied.

'And what do you think?'

'What do I think about what?' I asked.

'About Jehanne La Pucelle, the Maid. What do you think?'

I shrugged. 'She seems stubborn, loyal, aggressive, and has had a shattering effect upon the war.'

'You mean the fall of Orleans?'

I detected the tinge of anger in the speaker's voice. 'Yes, the fall of Orleans,' I mimicked the reply. Again the tip of the dagger nicked my throat. 'And what do *you* think?' I asked suddenly. 'Do you think she is a fiend of Satan, a limb of the devil?'

'She serves her master.' The reply was cool. 'And when she is finished, she will have to go to her allotted place.'

'Who is the master?' I asked, not frightened by the pool of silence around me. 'Does she serve the demons?'

'Perhaps. She is a good actress.' The voice continued, 'She can act any role. Look at her, Jankyn. In the name of God, she claims to be a saint but she kills men. She claims she is poor but she rejoices in silver and gilt armour, white surcoats, glorious banners and black destriers. She wishes to be accepted by the Dauphin and others of the French court. How can someone who comes from God rejoice in such luxury, such slaughter?'

'Very well, very well,' I murmured. 'What do you want of me?'

'Nothing.' Again I heard the snigger of the darkness and, even without seeing the person responsible, I felt a deep and lasting hatred for his malevolent mischievousness. 'We have simply come,' the voice continued, 'to introduce ourselves.'

'And your names?'

'Our names do not matter to you, Jankyn. To you, we are but shadows, yet we are always with you, always watching you, day and night.' The voice continued briskly, 'I know you must have wondered where we have been as this is the first time we have had the pleasure of each other's company, but we will stay with you wherever you go, whatever you do. Whether it is tumbling that pretty little widow at your lodging or fighting with the Maid, pretending to be the great hero on the battlefield. We will be there watching you. Remember that, Jankyn, and when we command, if you value your life, you will carry out certain tasks assigned to you and deliver the Maid into our hands.'

I was going to reply but I was picked up by a strong pair of arms. A door opened and I felt the night air on my face. I was then hurried down the streets with my feet slipping on the shit-stained cobbles. I was turned round, made a little dizzy and left to stagger. My hands went up the cloak around my head and I pulled it off to gulp in the cool night air. I looked around but there was nobody. Behind me was the long, dark street and before me a crossroads in the city. A statue of that quarter was in its niche lit by a great candle. There was also the remains of a bonfire which had been part of the celebrations for the city's deliverance from the English.

Two beggars sat near it, for although it was high summer the nights still tended to be cold. I walked over to them and they looked up as I approached. They were both old, with seamed faces and dirty grey hair. One of them had lost a leg and the stench from both was terrible.

'Messieurs,' I began. 'Have you seen other people in this square?' They looked at me blankly. 'Other people,' I repeated. 'Am I the only man to pass this way in the last few minutes?'

'You are the only man that has passed this way,' one of them replied caustically.

I peered closer and noticed the scabs on the man's wrinkled face and the blackened, yellow stumps as his lips parted. I withdrew in horror. For all I knew they might have been lepers. They could be of no assistance to me, so I left them.

That night, I did not even talk to my widow friend but walked off in a sulk, ignoring her pleas without even the slightest kiss. I brushed aside her anxious solicitations about food and drink and where I had been. Instead, I locked and barred the door of my room, sat on my bed and tried to clear my thoughts. Apparently there were at least two and possibly three men in Orleans on strict orders from someone who knew Beaufort to watch and communicate with me when they thought fit. They seemed to know the city well, being able to pluck me from an alleyway, take me to a house, question me, release me and disappear with a cool affrontery. I did not know who they were. They had spoken in English with a slight trace of an accent. Sometimes they lapsed into French but again with a slight trace of an accent. They knew a great deal about the Maid and certainly did not see her as someone sent from God.

I was well acquainted with the Satanic covens spread throughout Europe. They included peasants who met in secret groves and the highest in the land. Even Henry V's mother, Joanna of Navarre, had been accused of being a sorceress and of dabbling in the black arts. Only her high position had prevented such serious charges being pressed to their logical conclusion. I wondered if Jehanne was a witch. Was she a deceiver?

I remembered what Delon had told me about her past. Her father was a mere farmer and her mother of peasant stock. They were nothing exceptional. Delon also told me that Jehanne often went to church in Domremy where there is a statue of St. Margaret, and had prayed before a statue of St. Michael in the nearby town of Belmont. He said she had heard the voices whenever the church bells rang. She lived a pious life but otherwise had not been distinguished by any notable contribution to the local community. So could she be a witch? Again, I racked my brains. There was something wrong with a woman from God who dressed in a man's clothing, killed other men, liked finery and the presence of the great ones of the land. The speaker who had questioned me earlier was right in his observations. Was she, however, a witch and what instructions would be given for her betrayal? I filled a goblet with wine, drank it hastily and filled it again. I shivered, feeling cold and frightened. What was I to do? Betray the Maid? To do so might be betraying a saint, a personal friend of God, and, although I do not talk to God much, I do believe He exists. His power is ever pervasive and His memory eternal. What if Jankyn were to damn himself with a crime similar to that of Judas?

# TEN

The next morning, I joined Jehanne's retinue as the army assembled to leave Orleans and continue its march up the Loire. Alençon, the Dauphin's leading general, had now joined us. He commanded the army but the Maid exercised a great deal of influence with him. Our force was a mixed bag: a company of surgeons with carts and medicines by the sackful, coffers of herbs, knives and swords for amputations, leeches and irons for letting blood from men already weakened by its loss, rolls of linen bandages and salves from the juice of flowers which would make men drowsy when their wounds had to be tended after battle. There were also smiths and saddlers; tent-makers; baggage boys, no more than mere children, who guarded the horses and gear while their masters went on foot into combat; and hundreds of light horsemen or hobelars who were used as messengers or spies. Then, of course, there were the great knights, many of them with their own small baggage-train which carried their metal-plated armour, brigandines, basinets, helmets, gussets of chain-mail, swords, swordbelts, axes, daggers and pole-axes. Most of this was piled high in the wagons with the knights preferring to wear their quilted tunics of boiled leather which were moulded to the wearer's shape and stuffed, for added protection, with silk flock or cotton. In addition, there were some Genoese foot-soldiers, mercenaries who specialised in the use of the crossbow, a wicked-looking weapon which could fire quarrels of iron and steel. Less well-armed but equally savage was a large contingent of Irishmen whose only weapons were enormous knives and a bundle of short throwing-spears. Small, wild, bearded, permanently in love with war and death, they were disdained by most of the French forces. The Irish fought for the sheer love of it as well as the sacks of gold and prospects of ransom.

This ragged army assembled in the fields outside Orleans. I wondered if the Maid, even with Alençon present, could win the allegiance of such an army which was comprised of every nationality and type. I also met de Couzac. He greeted me briefly, being rather cold and distant. I wondered if it was jealousy on his part or perhaps fear of anyone who had come into close contact with the Maid. Indeed, I had noticed that, although the Maid was cheered and revered like some sacred symbol of the army, few people wanted to get close to her and most actually tended to stay out of her path. De Couzac reminded me of the rules I had agreed to adhere to when I joined the force. Any ransoms would have to be shared with the rest of the company and any plunder I took should, likewise, be directed to their carts for division. I agreed whole-heartedly, saying that so far I had had little chance to acquire wealth. I gave solemn assurances that when the occasion arose I would be open and fair with my comrades. De Couzac, like the fool he was, seemed to be convinced as he wandered off. If I stumbled on wealth then it would be for Master Jankyn and Master Jankyn alone. De Couzac, as far as I was concerned, could fly to heaven for divine support but still he would not get me to give in to him.

Eventually, the camp marshals got us into some form of order and instructions were issued. Every man was expected to be shriven and to take the sacrament. No women were to be allowed. The usual camp followers were banned and the Maid herself had decreed that any harlot coming within three miles of the camp would have her left arm broken. Swearing was forbidden. No insult was to be offered to any man, woman or child on the way and Jehanne reminded us that even the English had souls. Her sole intention was to drive them out of France and not to kill them. The army cheered her and the sky rang with the clamour, raising the birds, which swirled in wild flocks above us. The trumpets shrilled, the drums beat frenetically and the army, freshly provisioned, made its way out of Orleans towards Meung, a small town which was still held by the English and lay just down the river from Orleans.

There was a fortified bridge, garrisoned by the English, which kept the town secure. Under the Maid's direction, the French took the bridge and garrisoned it before skirting the town and marching against Beaugency further along the Loire. That night, the army camped in the fields, except for Alençon, who bivouacked in a nearby church. This decision nearly cost him his life. The English sent assassins across the river who got into the church. They would have stabbed the prince to death if it had not been for the vigilance of his bodyguard.

The next morning, as we left, we saw their bodies with their heads still covered in black hoods. They were swinging from the branch of a great elm tree which overlooked the route out of the camp. Four of the six assassins had been killed by Alençon's guard. The other two had been hanged alive and one of them was still kicking as the army passed the grisly scene. I watched the Maid carefully. I saw her face pale as we passed.

She looked neither to right nor left but, instead, gazed carefully down at the ring she wore on her hand. She fingered it as if that could remove from her mind the terrible vision of a man in his death-throes.

Our immediate objective was the fortress of Beaugency, a massive four-square donjon which commanded the Loire. The English garrison there had made the mistake of withdrawing from the town and securing themselves in the castle. They had left traps in the abbey buildings which lay just beneath them on the side of the hill. These were caltrops and mantraps, but the casualties they inflicted only inflamed the ardour of the French even more. A curious incident happened there. Our scouts brought us news that a French force was advancing under the banner of Arthur de Richemont, Constable of France. De Richemont had once been a favourite of the Dauphin, Charles, and, in fact, had been responsible for introducing La Tremoille into the royal household. La Tremoille's way of thanking Richemont was to ensure that the Dauphin and de Richemont quarrelled and Richemont was banned from the court forever.

The Maid and her captains did not know what Richemont meant by advancing. Was he going to attack them? Such a course of action would have been disastrous, but the problem was solved by the Maid and other captains going out to meet de Richemont. Jehanne knelt at the Constable's feet, embraced his legs and said he was most welcome as she had not asked him to come; but now he was here, she would use him for the great cause.

De Richemont seemed pleased by this action. I remember watching this group of great ones standing in a circle chatting.

Suddenly, the hands went out to be shaken. There were embraces, kisses of peace, and the whole group rejoined the main army.

The siege was now tightened and the English, seeing these fresh forces arrive and how close and secure was the circle of steel, asked for terms of surrender. Alençon, eager to continue the pursuit of the main English force as well as being fearful of another one appearing to relieve the fortress, agreed. His one condition was that the English captain, a sandy-haired, red-faced man named Matthew Gough, be held hostage for a while. The English were allowed to leave with horse and harness and a silver mark's worth of property. No sooner had the garrison marched out than our scouts brought news the following morning that John Falstaff and Gilbert Talbot, two of the most feared English commanders, were now advancing to meet us with a force of five thousand men. Panic broke out in the French camp. Some of the captains demanded an immediate retreat to Orleans but Jehanne calmed them. She swore that even if the English dangled from the skies they would be caught, since God now meant them to be chastised. She also said the French would gain their greatest victory for a long time. There would be few casualties and the French should wear their spurs, for they would need them.

Although we did not know it at the time (for Beaufort informed me of it later) the English milords were divided. Talbot demanded that the French should be brought to battle and destroyed but John Falstaff, more cautious and cunning, insisted that the English did not know the true size of the French forces or if the Maid led them. More importantly, the terrain to be covered was unsuitable for a pitched battle. Fortunately for the French, Falstaff lost the argument and the English came on. Both armies marched criss-cross over the plain of Beauce. Falstaff was right, the terrain was unsuitable for any close battle. It was heavily wooded, with dips and rises, covered by hedgerows, and because of the ravages of war all cultivation had disappeared. Nature had reclaimed its own. Eventually, both armies met. Alençon commanded that Jehanne, much to her disgust, should stay in the rear while the French deployed on a small rise above the main road which ran alongside the Loire.

The English came up with their standards fluttering in the breeze which carried the sound of their trumpets and drumbeats. They took up their usual deployment for battle. Horsemen dismounted and stakes were driven into the ground with archers behind them waiting for us to attack. Alençon was too cunning for this ploy. He had learnt from the mistakes of Agincourt, so he simply sat and waited. Eventually, a horseman left the English ranks. Galloping in a cloud of dust towards the French, he shouted how the English were now waiting for the French to come on. If the French were frightened the English would send out three men to see if the French had the courage to come down and meet them. Such arrogance was intended to provoke us into battle but Alençon kept calm, pointing out it was now late and that tomorrow, with God and Our Lady helping them, the French would advance and take a closer look.

Perhaps the cool audacity of such a reply disturbed the English leaders. Did Alençon, they wondered, know something they did not? During the night, they found he did. News arrived stating that Beaugency had fallen and that de Richemont had joined the French force so that the army now facing them was much bigger than they had thought. Talbot and Falstaff immediately retreated and the Maid ordered a pursuit. I kept close to her retinue, right next to her standard-bearer. The French moved cautiously along the road, the scouts out searching among the dips and hedgerows and in the woods for any sign of the English force. All I can remember of that hot summer's morning is the army slowly moving along the road with columns and columns of men-at-arms, and the mounted knights in half-armour, the sweat trickling down their faces as if water had been thrown over them. The inside of my thighs chafed against the saddle, my throat was dry, and above us the sun threatened to become even hotter.

The countryside slept under a heavy summer haze. The last thing I wanted was a battle. Suddenly, a scout spurring along the road brought the whole army to life. Orders were issued. Men-at-arms put on their helmets again, tightened their belts and gripped their pikes. The knights began to call on their pages asking them to bring up their armour. Banners were unfurled. Trumpets called. The camp marshals hurried up and down, officious in their orders about the columns deploying in their proper order of march. The Maid was very eager. I rode up alongside and watched. Her face white with excitement, her lips tense, she kept running her fingers through her short, cropped hair, impatient for the messenger to reach her.

The news he brought was quite extraordinary. The English were hidden further along the road in fields, taking up a position between two narrow hedgerows. The scouts had apparently stumbled on them because of a stag which the English had surprised. When it fled, the English gave a great roar which brought them to the notice of the French. Alençon heard the scout's report and quietly issued orders that the entire French army should debouch off the road and advance through the heavy wooded land, towards the area where the scouts had established the enemy's position.

The English had encamped just outside the small town of Patay and what followed was one of the strangest battles I have ever been involved in or heard about. The English had been in four divisions. However, due to the rivalry between the two leaders, Talbot and Falstaff, orders were not eagerly obeyed and communications were poor. Talbot, leading the first division, began to deploy his archers but the wagon-train, further along the line, had to be turned and brought back to the position Talbot had chosen. At the very moment that he was trying to deploy his archers, La Hire with a handful of men took the English in the flanks. Talbot was immediately captured and his archers, unable to use their fearsome longbows and wicked-edged arrows, were cut down to a man.

Falstaff was midway between divisions. He saw what was happening to Talbot and immediately rode back to try and get the rest of the English army to stand. The army thought he was fleeing and, following suit, set spur and left the English foot to the mercy of the French. What followed was a massacre. The unfortunates, betrayed by their leaders and captains, simply stood there whilst the French horsemen wove in between them like a needle through tapestry, cutting and hacking them down. Soon the fields outside Patay were filled with the cries of screaming, dying men. I was behind the Maid and I can swear I never struck a blow though what I saw was merciless.

Without their leaders, the English had not been ordered into any phalanx or deployment. Some of the more intelligent tried to form circles or squares whilst a few of the archers set up a line for the rest to hide behind, but it was useless. The French simply cut them down. I saw men-at-arms and archers wheel away with hands at their faces to cover the great, jagged, blood-spouting wounds. In some places, the English dead lay in heaps like bundles of faggots cut and hewn by an expert woodsman. The Maid, white-faced at what she saw, leaned over her horse and vomited. She then rode up to La Hire and Alençon screaming at them to stop the killing.

Gradually, the French camp marshals managed to impose order. The English prisoners were herded into groups and their hands bound. They were then ordered to march back to the main road. One of the French, a mercenary, perhaps realising that his capture was not worth any ransom, suddenly took out a club and smashed an Englishman on his head. The man fell to the ground. The Maid, seeing this incident, rode up and screamed abuse at the French mercenary before dismounting and holding the wounded man's head in her lap, comforting him and making him confess his sins.

La Hire's horsemen followed the remnants of the enemy army back to Angerville which was still held by the English. However, the castle had been left in the hands of a young squire who, as soon as he heard of the defeat of the English army, immediately entered into negotiations with a view to surrender. A verbal treaty was soon reached in which the squire promised to behave as a good and loyal Frenchman and the small castle was handed over to La Hire. It was a rich prize, containing artillery, war equipment, foodstuffs and even Falstaff's war-chest full of silver and gold coin. Poor Falstaff had no choice but to continue his flight to Corbeil, where an enraged Duke of Bedford stripped him of the Order of the Garter and ordered him to be kept under house-arrest before sending him home in disgrace. Eventually, however, Bedford relented. He realised that the defeat at Patay had been caused, not by Falstaff, but by the violent temper and pride of Gilbert Talbot.

On the night after the battle, we entered the town of Patay where the townspeople held a great banquet in our honour. We sat in a small guildhall before tables covered with white lawn and silver ornaments winking and glittering in the light of hundreds of candles placed in great iron candelabra around the room. At the beginning of the feast, Talbot, who had been captured in the battle, was brought before the French commanders. The Maid he ignored and, for once, she was quiet. Alençon, however, unable to contain himself, announced that he could not believe the French had gained such a victory. Talbot, grey-haired and with a face of iron containing large, deep-set eyes and a cruel rat-trap of a mouth, managed to contain himself. He answered gruffly that it was the fortunes of war, and, looking meaningfully at the Maid, said there would be another day.

# ELEVEN

As I said, I had taken part in the battle of Patay, but, whilst being entranced by the Maid and her pervasive influence, I could not bring myself to kill fellow-countrymen in such a cold-blooded manner. I came out of the fracas unscathed except for a knock on the head which, at first, I dismissed. However, the following day I fell ill with a fever. Delon found me sweating and delirious in one of the out-stables of a house where the Maid was staying. Thanks to his kindness and generosity, I was returned to Orleans and the widow's house on a makeshift stretcher. The journey was a nightmare. Sometimes, in my thoughts, I was back in England, and at other times in some gold-enriched chamber with Beaufort sitting on a throne with the Maid next to him smiling evilly at me. Ghosts from the past, both men and women whom I had loved or hated, all crowded in, eager to seize my soul.

Looking back on the pages I have written, or rather what this cantankerous little priest has written, I apologise if I have given the impression that the widow in Orleans was a little trollop. She was more than that. She was kind and loving. A few days after my return to her house the fever abated, but I was still in a weak state. The widow put the infection down to bad food and drinking dirty water. I just wondered whether it was a sickness of the mind, with my blood and humours turning at what I had seen, coupled with anxiety about my future. I lay ill at Orleans for weeks with the widow tending me with potions, herbs, hot soups and good, white bread. I begged her, whenever I gained consciousness, not to allow any physician near me. She smiled and nodded. Speaking softly to me in French, she wiped the top of my brow like a mother does with a child.

I have always dreaded doctors. They know as much about the human body and the human spirit as a gnat! If I had my way, I would herd them, together with lawyers, and put them all in the country's gaols. I notice the priest who is transcribing this looks at me strangely. If he is not careful, I will add that I believe the same fate should await priests. I cannot stand any of them. Anyhow, I wander. The fever finally broke but I was as weak as a babe, fit only for sitting up in bed or walking very carefully around my room. I think it is only now, whilst looking back down the years, that I realise how close I was to death. I sometimes wonder if I had been poisoned, for I have a stout physique and a strong body. The suddenness of the illness and the effect upon me was quite horrid.

I listened to rumours of how the Maid had persuaded the Dauphin to go to Rheims for consecration. I could understand this, for no French king can be considered as one unless he has been anointed by the holy oil given direct by God. If the Maid achieved this then the English cause in France was indeed finished. In a few months, she had turned a shambling young man, who was considering flight to Spain or Scotland, into a king. The Maid was, indeed, successful. At the end of July, I received a letter from Delon not written in his hand but, possibly, by one of the priests. I still have the greasy yellow parchment and, when I read it now, I am back in that room in Orleans receiving tidings about events which surprised the rest of Europe.

'Jean Delon, Squire to the Maid, to Master Matthias

Jankyn residing in Orleans, health and greetings. My mistress sends you her good wishes. She asks you to be of good heart so that you will recover soon from your sickness and be able to join us again. The news is still very good. The victory at Patay is a sure sign that God is with us and favours our cause. The Maid has been to see His Grace, the Dauphin, at Senlis and other places. She tells him to have no doubt that he would gain his whole kingdom and soon be crowned. However, there are those around the King who now fear the Maid and see her army, which has now swollen to twelve thousand, as a direct threat to the Crown. This must, indeed, be the work of Satan. The Maid's task is simply to support the Dauphin to become King of France and drive the English out. People are saying how La Tremoille and others of the King's Council are very angry that the Maid has attracted so many people and they even fear for their own persons.

'Nevertheless, due to God's good grace, the Maid, together with the Duke of Alençon, persuaded the Dauphin to go to Rheims. Those who opposed His Grace leaving said the road was still blocked by English-held forts, but the Maid persuaded the Dauphin that such places would surrender. However, so malignant are the English and their allies, the town of Auxerre held out. The Maid was angry when she heard that the townspeople had paid La Tremoille over two thousand ecus for the place not to be stormed. Troyes, however, did surrender. Here, the Maid met Brother Richard who had recently returned from the Holy Land, prophesying that the Antichrist had been born. He and my mistress have now become close and fast friends which is another sign that the Maid is accepted by God.

'The Maid's prophecy about being accepted at Rheims has also proved true. On the 16th July, a delegation came from the city to bring the Dauphin both the keys and their submission. This act was greeted with great joy not only by the Maid but by the Dauphin and Archbishop Regnault to whom Charles had given Rheims. Regnault, however, had never had the chance to enter the city because of the Goddamns' possession. That same day, the Archbishop entered his city for the first time. In the evening the Dauphin made his own entry accompanied by the Maid and the whole army. The crowds packed the streets shouting "Noel" at our approach.

'At first, there was great confusion; the royal regalia for the coronation was kept at St. Denis, near Paris, which is still in English hands, but the Maid insisted that we would have to use what we could find. At three o'clock the next morning, the Dauphin entered the cathedral to keep the traditional vigil before he was anointed. At nine, the church doors were opened and the coronation, blessed by God, began. After the singing of the Divine Office and the "Veni Creatus Spiritus", four knights in full armour were sent on horseback, each carrying his banner, to fetch the holy ampulla containing the sacred oil from the church of St. Remi. A short while afterwards, they returned escorting the Abbot of St. Remi carrying the ampulla. You will not have seen this object. It is a beautiful glass flask enclosed in the belly of a golden dove which has claws and feet of coral. It was, indeed, wonderfully turned, for the bird, fitted with plates made of silver and gilt and studded with precious stones, hung by a chain from the Abbot's neck. He was mounted on a horse draped in the costliest velvet and above him was borne a canopy of the purest cloth of gold. Escorted by the four knights, the Abbot rode up the great steps of the cathedral and down the nave as far as the choir. Here, the Archbishop of Rheims, attended by the canons of the church, took the ampulla and placed it on the high altar.

'The King then swore the oath to keep the peace of

the church, protect the people and govern with justice and mercy before being knighted by Alençon. I was with Jehanne in the sanctuary and watched the whole splendour and mystery of the glorious occasion. The Archbishop blessed the royal ornaments and anointed the King kneeling before him. When this was finished, the crown was raised and placed gently on the Dauphin's head. The crowd cried "Noel" and the trumpets sounded so loud I thought the very vaults of the church would split. During the whole ceremony, the Maid stood beside the King holding her standard in her hand. Indeed, it was a fine thing to see the way in which the King and Maid conducted themselves. When Jehanne saw the King was consecrated and crowned, she knelt before him in the presence of all the lords and said these words to him, embracing him by the knees and weeping hot tears:

' "Gentle King, now is fulfilled the pleasure of God who wished that the siege of Orleans should be lifted and that you should be brought into the city of Rheims to receive your holy consecration, thus showing that you are true King and he to whom the kingdom of France should belong." All who saw this action were deeply moved.

'After the ceremony, a great banquet was held in the Archbishop's palace at which the Lords Alençon and Clermont and other principal lords were present to serve the King. After this, His Grace, wearing his crown and accompanied by the Maid, went round the city to show himself to the people who were as desirous to see her as to touch the King.

'Know you also that the King has made a truce with the Duke of Burgundy which is to last for fifteen days. The Duke has promised to surrender the city of Paris peacefully at the end of the fifteenth day. The Maid is not content with this truce and believes that Burgundy will play us false. She has remonstrated with the King to march on Paris, take those towns which lie in between, and bring the Duke of Bedford to battle to destroy him. The self-styled Regent of England and France sent a most insulting letter to our King stating thus:

' "You, who used to call youself the Dauphin of Viennois and now, without cause, say you are King. Know you that I will pursue and continue to pursue you from place to place.' Bedford continues: 'Therefore I challenge you to stand fast and be ready to give battle either in the land of Champagne and Brie or in the Île de France which is closer to us."

'The King, however, refused this challenge and marched on Senlis. The Duke of Bedford, on hearing this move, took up his position nearby, guarding his front in the usual manner with stakes, ditches and baggage-carts. All day the French and English tried to bring each other to battle. I was with the Maid when she rode up to the English front and, tapping her lance on their barricades, encouraged them to battle. They refused, so both armies sat and watched each other for two days. They then rose and circled each other like fighting dogs with hackles raised and mouths snarling. It was gruelling under the hot summer sun. The dust hung like a fog and in the skirmishes I found it difficult to distinguish friend from foe.

'During one of these skirmishes, La Tremoille, who had ridden up to the enemy in an attempt to imitate Jehanne, was almost captured when his horse slipped to the ground trapping him beneath it. For a while, the King's favourite risked being killed or captured by the English, until he was eventually rescued. After that, the English withdrew to Paris and Charles, unwilling to pursue to give battle, also retreated. The Maid was disconsolate at this action. If the French had brought Bedford to battle and defeated him, the English cause in France would have been lost.

'The Maid is in good spirits, however, although

privately she fears treachery. She says that her voices have told her that before next summer is out she will have been betrayed. She sends you her greetings as I do mine. Written at Senlis, August 1429.'

I remember putting the letter down and wishing that I was back in the Maid's retinue fighting against my own countrymen. My time with her had been like a dream, being cut off from England and Beaufort, from my past with all its agonies and betrayals and from the fact that I was a spy. I also felt alarmed because the Maid had talked about betrayal. I knew the web was being spun and, whoever the spiders were, they were intent on catching their prey.

There were other stories circulating about the Maid, such as about her high-handed attitude in requisitioning a horse from the Bishop of Senlis, in getting her family given noble status and her town exemption from taxes. She openly cultivated the people of Orleans and accepted presents from them as she did from other towns. The King, so rumours had it, feared the Maid might drive the English out of France and then turn on him. It was a fear nourished and cherished by La Tremoille like a gardener does a fragile, precious flower. I had heard other stories about how the Maid had broken the sword which she had fetched from the church of St. Catherine de Fierbois, snapping it on the back of some poor camp follower she had chased from the army. Also, how the common people had nicknamed her 'L'Angelique', the Angelic One, and made her the subject of popular songs and sermons. Even miracles were placed at her door. Some people called her greater than all the saints of God after the Blessed Virgin, putting up images and representations of her in the basilicas and carrying medals struck in her honour, as if she was a canonised saint or an angel rather than a woman.

Despite King Charles' objections, the Maid insisted on

recapturing Paris. She and the Duke of Alençon arrived at St. Denis, just outside Paris, on the 25th August to find part of the walls had been thrown down, the moat filled up and the most important citizens withdrawn to Paris. A series of skirmishes took place outside La Chapelle, a little village which lay on the main road to Paris.

The Parisians, however, were reluctant to welcome Jehanne and began to organise their defences. Bedford poured money and men into the city. He realised that if it was lost the English cause would suffer a serious blow and it would be further proof of the Maid's divine mission. Guns were brought up and placed on the ramparts of the city. Barrels full of stones were made ready as were huge vats full of boiling oil. The moat was repaired and barricades were raised to divide one quarter from another. Chains were hung across the narrow streets to bring down horsemen. The English behaved bravely, fortifying the walls and marching up and down the ramparts with banners displayed and trumpets blowing.

On the 8th September, Jehanne and Alençon launched their first assault against Paris. From the beginning, it did not prove well. As usual, the Maid led the assault, crossing one of the ditches and testing the other filled with water. Here she shouted out to the Parisians:

'Surrender to us quickly in Jesus' name. If you do not surrender before nightfall, we shall come in by force and you will all be killed.'

A bowman, on hearing this, bellowed back, 'Shall we, you bloody tart?'

He then took aim with his arbalest and put a bolt straight into the fleshy part of her thigh. The Maid collapsed and, although she wanted to stay, had to be dragged back to her lines.

The sight of Jehanne's fall cheered the Parisians and

the English garrison whilst depressing her own men, so the attack began to falter. The King, hearing of this, ordered a withdrawal and the Maid, bitter and angry at not taking the capital as she had prophesied, had to agree. The news spread despair in Orleans for their great heroine had both been wounded and proved wrong. I wondered if the Maid's luck had begun to change. She was alienated from the King, her magical sword had been broken, she had failed to capture Paris as prophesied, and now she was wounded. I felt sorry for her and I found this strange. Usually, I don't care a fig for anyone!

# TWELVE

One night, just after I received news about the Maid's withdrawal from Paris, I was woken when the house was silent and dark. Someone was in my room. I fumbled for a tinder to strike the candle which stood on a stool beside my bed, but at the foot of the bed, a flare was struck and a candle flared into light. Whoever had done it, and I suspected there were two in the room, knew that the light would both rivet my attention and give them greater concealment. I could see shadows deeper than the rest at the end of the room.

'Master Jankyn,' the voice began smoothly. 'Do not touch the tinder or cry out or look for the dagger which we know lies by the side of your bed! We have a crossbow bolt aimed directly at your chest.'

I heard the angry click of the winch being pulled back and knew that the speaker was not bluffing.

'Who are you?' I said testily.

'We are the Shadows,' the voice replied, sounding like an indulgent father talking to a spoilt child. 'We have come, Master Jankyn, to see how you are.'

'I am well,' I replied sardonically. 'Why this visit at the dead of night? Why cannot you meet me in the full light of day?'

'Soon, soon,' the voice soothingly replied, caricaturing scripture, 'things which are hid in darkness, done in the night, will be revealed in the full glare of day. For the time being, our masters think it is proper that we

111

should meet this way.' I heard the malevolent giggling again and knew that deep in the shadows there was a second figure.

'Your friend,' I said, 'he laughs a lot. What does he find so amusing?'

'Oh,' the speaker replied, 'he would like to kill you, but I tell him you have things to do. The French bitch, the Armagnac whore, the harlot calling herself the Maid, she has deviated from the Master's task.'

'Which Master?' I interjected. 'Satan?'

'Never mind that,' the voice came again. 'Her day will come at Compiegne.'

'Compiegne?' I had heard of the town on the road to Paris which was of vital concern to both the Burgundians and French. Whoever controlled it would control the routes into the city. 'What will happen at Compiegne?'

'Make sure,' the speaker replied, 'make sure that the Maid does not attack, that she is kept there. You do understand?'

'What does that mean?' I asked.

The candle went out. I heard a slither of soft leather and by the time I had got up from my bed the Shadows were gone. I knew pursuit was futile. I opened the small, horn-glazed window and looked up at a clear, frost-hardened autumn sky. Beneath me, the narrow street was quiet and, despite the chill breeze, I stood staring out over the darkening city wondering who these Shadows were and why they had come. I shivered not just because of the cold but because they maintained that the Maid was to be betrayed and had actually named the place. I made a decision, irrespective of the mission Beaufort had assigned me, to rejoin the Maid as soon as possible and do what I could to save her from her intended fate.

I rejoined her at Bourges at the end of October. She seemed ill at ease in the marble corridors and silk-draped chambers of the princes and missed her brother-in-arms, Alençon, who was now campaigning in Normandy. Her other captains, including La Hire, had been directed towards other duties. Delon greeted me with pleasure. The Maid, again, just looked strangely at me, nodded and smiled. Her face was white and drawn as if she had been through some great tragedy. She seemed fidgety and was constantly on the move, unable to rest or relax. Even I could see the King was beginning to tire of her.

Jehanne now wished to launch an attack upon St. Pierre le Moutiere, held by a freebooter named Gressart. A mason by trade, he had been a leader of mercenaries for the last ten years in the full pay of the Duke of Burgundy. Indeed, so impudent had he become that four years earlier he had even seized La Tremoille and made the Court pay his ransom. Perhaps in an attempt to placate La Tremoille, who was denying the Maid both money and resources, a plan was formed. St. Pierre itself is small, being no more than a village huddled tightly around a church. The Maid was given a professional soldier, Alberet, to help her, together with a force composed mainly of foreign mercenaries to take it.

On the 2nd November, the feast of All Souls, on a heavy, overcast day with a thick mist creeping in from the river, the Maid launched her attack. The Burgundian force resisted fiercely and seemed intent on fighting from house to house. Their crossbow men were particularly keen and accurate. They managed to stop our advance with a hail of vicious quarrels and bolts, one of which injured Delon in the heel so that he was forced to retire. He subsequently walked for a long time on crutches. This incident left the Maid virtually exposed, for Delon always followed her into battle. I, therefore, decided to keep close to her. So far, I had prided myself that in all the fighting I had been well protected by Jehanne, but then I saw something which totally mystified me.

The Maid had advanced against a house which was strongly fortified by the enemy. I mounted a horse and rushed towards her to ask what she was doing alone, why she had not retired with the rest, for the mercenaries had broken and run in the face of such fierce opposition. The Maid took her helmet off. She seemed distant, pale, impervious to what was going on around her, and loudly declared she was not alone, she still had fifty thousand men in her company and she would not leave the spot until she had taken it.

'Madame,' I said, 'where are these fifty thousand? There are only the two of us and the enemy in the house is taking aim against us.'

She spun round on me tight-lipped and ordered faggots and withies to be sent for, to make a bridge over the moat so we might get nearer the house. I just stared at her, so she ran back down the cobbled street and shouted:

'Faggots, withies, everybody, so we can make a bridge!' Surprisingly, these items were brought and put into position. The whole affair utterly astonished me. Jehanne's mercenaries regrouped and crossed. The house was taken and within an hour the entire town had fallen.

Later that day, I wondered what the Maid had meant by the fifty thousand. Was she insane? Did she really believe a great army was supporting her? Was she talking about a heavenly host or a demon army? I felt sorry for her and wondered if she was beginning to lose her wits. But the reality we all saw was being perceived in a totally different way by her. From Le Moutiere, we moved on to the siege of La Charite, but, after bombarding this town, we had to withdraw for La Tremoille did not send us the necessary supplies and the Maid had to write to other towns, begging for

powder, arrows and other supplies of war. Some of
these towns, including Orleans, responded generously
but with not enough for the Maid to continue her
campaigns.

After this, the Maid was finished. She returned to
Bourges and spent the winter listlessly moving from one
palace to another. Delon, myself and a few others
followed her. She also began to quarrel with Brother
Richard. He was the eccentric friar who claimed he had
been to the Holy Land and met Jews in their thousands
moving towards Babylon to greet the birth of the
antichrist. He was an excellent speaker but I think he
was a rogue with a golden tongue. I can always
recognise a kindred spirit. Moreover, he had with him a
young girl, Catherine, who also claimed to be a
visionary.

The Maid, now denied any support and treated like a
mascot by the Court, was drawn into Brother Richard's
circle. She listened to silly stories told by Catherine
about a white lady, clad in gold, who came to the
visionary telling her she should travel through towns
and that the King should give her heralds and trumpets
to have it announced that anyone having gold, silver or
hidden treasure should bring it out at once. Those in
possession of such goods hidden away who did not
produce them, would be found out by Catherine. Such a
scheme, the visionary said, would pay the Maid's
men-at-arms. When I heard this, I laughed until I was
pained. Indeed, a marvellous plan! Catherine, travelling through the towns asking for gold and silver which,
I strongly suspected, would end up in her coffers and
that of Brother Richard rather than any of the Maid's.

So angry, however, did Jehanne become with
Richard's visionary that she insisted that Catherine and
she sleep in the same bed so they both could see the
famous white lady. Jehanne, in fact, watched until
midnight but saw nothing. Afterwards, she slept. When

morning came, the Maid asked Catherine if the lady had come. Catherine said yes but it had been whilst Jehanne slept and Catherine had been unable to waken her. The Maid, therefore, rested the whole of the next day so as to be able to watch the entire night, but again nothing happened. To give her credit, Jehanne realised Catherine was a fake and quarrelled violently with Brother Richard over it. Delon, hearing of these events, asked the Maid if she would let him see the saints who came to counsel her. She replied:

'You are not sufficiently worthy or virtuous to see them.' Then, turning on me, added, 'You Jankyn, would certainly betray them.'

I returned her hard stare coolly whilst trying to control the trembling in my body. I had begun to dread this woman who, on occasion, acted like a stupid peasant but on others as a dangerous visionary. I could never make my mind up as to which Jehanne was.

Women like Catherine are common. You see them in any fairground touting for business. She was later brought to trial and confessed to errors. She escaped with her life but others did not. Pierron, a visionary from Brittany, claimed to have visions. She, however, stuck to her beliefs and was burned in Paris on the 3rd September, 1430. Perhaps it is important to realise that the Maid was only one of many visionaries who plagued France trying to catch the attention of the King and Court. La Tremoille was a cunning, evil bastard and his master, Charles VII, a weak-kneed, feckless young man. Both were pestered by visionaries. Even Regnault, Archbishop of Rheims, had a shepherd-boy named Guevedan who also claimed to have been sent by God. When the English captured him, they paid the boy little heed and drowned him in a nearby river. As I have said, the French Court was besieged by visionaries. If the French had had as many good generals as they had prophets, the English would have been driven out of

France within a year. Jehanne's tragedy was that she was not one of the suspect seers, but she shared the fate meted out to them.

By the end of March, the first threads of the great tragedy were being sewn. I also heard the astonishing news that Cardinal Beaufort and the young Henry VI of England had landed at Calais and were awaiting safe passage down to Paris and Rouen. Our good Cardinal had been commissioned by Pope Martin V to raise an army and take it to Bohemia to fight the Hussite heretics. Beaufort, the arch schemer, took the gold, raised the army and immediately took it to France to help the English cause. By doing so, he managed to silence his opponents at home as well as winning the support of the English in France. He was a cunning serpent for now that the young King was in France Bedford's regency lapsed. If the regency lapsed, then the young King ruled and, of course, Beaufort ruled the King. From a letter smuggled to me in Orleans, I learnt that Beaufort wished to see me. God knows how it arrived for I simply found it in my room. Perhaps it had been brought by the Shadows. The note was cryptic enough.

'Your master,' it read, 'believes you have been away from home too long and it is time you returned to account for your stewardship.'

I should think so as well. Most of the silver Beaufort had given me I had either spent or lodged with bankers in some of the French towns. I suppose one always has to take care of the future and so much silver was too much of a temptation for me.

The Maid, also, reasserted herself at the end of March. There was a captain, a Burgundian called Franque Derras, who had served long in the wars in the service of the Duke of Burgundy. This Franque had organised a small army of mercenaries who raided French possessions taking men, women and children, as

well as booty, for Franque's use. At the beginning of
April, he launched such a raid. He had about three
hundred men with him. The Maid heard of Franque's
activities when she was at Lagny and immediately
decided to deal with him for she was full of frustration
at the obstacles placed before her. She had four
hundred men-at-arms and was aided by a Scotsman
called Sir Hugh Kennedy, as well as a Piedmontese
mercenary called Bartholomew Barreta. With their
advice, the Maid left Lagny with her force and trapped
Franque as he was returning from his raiding mission.
He was unable to escape because of the booty he was
carrying. So he dismounted his men in meadows
bordering the river Marne and ranged them beside a
hedge deploying archers to protect them.

I was with the Maid when she made two assaults on
the hedge, slashing, cutting and beating back the
helmeted faces before us. However, the Maid used her
brain this time, not just her emotions. She sent back to
Lagny where her old friend, another French captain
called Ambrose de Lorraine, was staying. She begged
him to bring up reinforcements which he did. Franque
was surrounded and surrendered, happy to be
ransomed. The Maid, however, had recently been part
of a conspiracy to raise a revolt in Paris which had failed
in its endeavour. Some of the leaders there had been
executed by the English, so the Maid, because of this act,
refused Franque ransom. She ordered him to be tried
by her own captains and executed. It was a summary
act. Franque, pale-faced and with his black straggly hair
framing thin, emaciated features, begged for mercy,
going down on his knees when he realised that the old
conventions of war had failed. The Maid was im-
placable. Franque was a freebooter, a traitor, a plun-
derer and a rapist. She sentenced him to death. He was
hurried out of the court into the market-place of
Lagny where his head was placed on a block of wood.

The master swordsman took it off his body clean at the neck and tumbled it into the basket while the neck spewed red plumes of blood. The Maid watched the execution white-faced and tight-lipped, before turning away to say the 'Miserere' for the mercenary's benighted soul.

A short while after this, the town of Melun surrendered and the Maid took it in the name of King Charles of France. She went up to the battlements, as she was accustomed to do, to catch the evening air and I caught her there, huddled in a corner of the stonework.

'Madame,' I said, 'what is the matter?'

She looked up, with her deep, dark, peasant eyes glaring balefully at me.

'I am to be betrayed and it will be soon,' she said. I tried to soothe her but she turned away.

That evening, in Melun, the Shadows returned. I was sleeping in a small outhouse when they arrived. Again, they struck a candle and stayed before me so that the light glared into my eyes and hid their appearances.

'Master Jankyn,' they said. 'The Burgundians are to besiege Compiegne. Make sure she stays in the town, we beg you. Then we will have her and your task will be completed.'

The Shadows vanished. God knows I never saw them but I hated their sinister elusiveness, these shadows in the night, these clouds before a midday sun. I was also sorry for the Maid. Deserted by the King and hampered by La Tremoille, she was like a bird trapped in the house with her wings beating and her breast heaving at the imprisonment enforced upon her. Anyway, as I have said, the tragedy began to unfurl. It was centred on Compiegne which was the city the Shadows had mentioned. Looking back, I believe there were forces at work. Dark, sinister ones, pushing the Maid towards a certain spot in time and history for the tragedy to be enacted. I knew Beaufort wanted me back but I was determined to stay to the bitter end.

Compiegne is a pleasant, walled, market-town which then controlled the routes into Paris as it does now. Whoever holds Compiegne can threaten Paris so, naturally, both the French King and Burgundy saw the market town as a vital location. King Charles had even offered it to Burgundy in a series of failed peace negotiations but the citizens of the town rose in rebellion against this suggestion and said they would not accept Burgundy. The Duke, furious at such a response, now vented his own personal spite by besieging Compiegne and in this he was aided by the English.

The Maid prepared to move her forces to the town, despite my personal warnings not to do so. She just looked at me strangely. At the time, she was in a deep depression. She even woke up at night, so Delon told me, to pace the floor and cry out that she would be betrayed with the traitors closing in around her. She attempted to quarter her troops in the nearby city of Soissons but the garrison commander there had already sold the city to the Burgundians. The Maid, therefore, had to disband many of her troops, keeping only four hundred around her, as Compiegne could not quarter a large army.

I often wondered whether the captain in Soissons had been paid to go over to the Burgundians, knowing full well the effect that action would have on the Maid's army. I remembered what the Shadows had told me, that as long as the Maid was in Compiegne she was safe. I therefore counselled her, time and time again, not to leave the town, but to stay within the defences. She brusquely interrupted me, however, and told me that her guidance was not from people like myself but came direct from God.

I suppose there is very little one can do in the face of such female arrogance. With the four hundred men, we

made our way through the thick woodland around
Compiegne and arrived in the town just before dawn on
the 24th May. Around us, the Burgundian army which
consisted of up to six thousand Burgundians, Picardes
and some English, guarded the far bank from
Compiegne across the river Oise. We were welcomed by
the commander, an old war-horse called Guyonne de
Flavel who had a foxy face and shifty eyes. I did not
trust him but there again I do not think he betrayed us.
He, too, cautioned the Maid immediately she arrived at
his headquarters, telling her not to attempt any of her
impetuous sallies from the town. Delon and I also tried
to restrain her but the Maid was adamant. She had
brought a force of four hundred men; she intended to
launch an attack upon the minor outposts which the
enemy had set up around the town.

'Do your voices say that?' I taunted.

'My voices,' she replied coolly, 'have ordered me to
drive the English out of France. We are here in
Compiegne, a vital town of our lord, the King,
surrounded by the King's enemies. It is only right that
we go out and attempt to clear them from the field.'

All day I vainly struggled to persuade her to have
nothing to do with Compiegne and return to the royal
headquarters, but the Maid was stubborn. Late in the
afternoon, she organised her force. Dressed in her
silver armour covered by floating panels of a gorgeous
gold and scarlet surcoat, she mounted a very beautiful
and fiery dapple-grey horse to lead her men out of
Compiegne to attack a nearby Burgundian post.

A slight breeze had arisen which cooled the heat of
the day as Jehanne, banner snapping before her,
rushed her force right into the Burgundian camp where
the soldiers, mostly disarmed and resting after the
fatigue of the day, were totally unprepared for the
assault. As we left, however, (and I was riding behind
her), the church bells of Compiegne had begun to toll as

if somebody was giving a signal that the Maid was launching an attack. At first, I took no notice. After all, it was eventide and the chimes could be dismissed as a call to prayer. Looking back, I now realise a traitor in the town was telling the enemy the Maid was leaving. This action proved to be her downfall.

# THIRTEEN

The Maid had launched a surprise attack but the bell aroused Burgundians, English and Picardes to assemble their forces and send fresh troops to the aid of the outpost under assault. The end was very near. The Maid was fighting furiously in the middle of the mêlée. I was next to her, shouting and exclaiming, my sword rising and falling though I did not care whom it hit.

I guided my horse expertly to keep myself away from any threat of real attack. Suddenly the enemy reinforcements arrived and we were pushed back towards Compiegne. I seized the Maid's bridle and begged her:

'Madame, we must leave, we must leave. The enemy is too great!' The Maid, visor up, looked around wildly and said:

'I have enough men here.'

'You have not,' I snapped. 'You must return!'

We then began a nightmare-like gallop back towards the drawbridge and into the city. As we travelled, we encountered solitary enemy horsemen who attempted to block our way. I, like the Maid and others around her, brushed them aside, screaming at the castle guards before us not to raise the drawbridge, as the Maid was returning. They may have heard my cry but totally rejected it, for as we continued that mad gallop, the ground flying underneath our horses' hooves, the drawbridge began to rise. I screamed, cursed and yelled. My horse, a full charger, gathered pace and, with one great bound, leapt with a crash on to its wooden slats and I was safely within the protection of the gate.

'Lower the drawbridge!' I screamed, but the man ignored me and the winching continued. I looked around thinking the Maid had followed me and I noticed in horror how her horse had become bogged down in the marshy ground around the moat. I turned my horse back but someone seized the bridle and I was pulled gently from it.

'It is too late,' a voice rasped in French. 'You can do nothing for her.' I pushed him away and ran up the narrow spiral staircase to the crenellated top of the gate-tower and looked down. I saw the Maid, now surrounded by enemy foot-soldiers, her beautiful standard lowered, her surcoat flapping in the wind as she tried to turn her horse and break out of the circle. I saw a pair of hands pluck her from the saddle. The horse was led away and the mob closed in. I slumped on the battlements, pushing my fist into my mouth trying to hold back my tears. The Maid was taken.

Eventually I composed myself, my sorrow now replaced by a deep anger. Someone had betrayed us. They had waited for the Maid to leave and had sounded the tocsin, alarming all the enemy outposts. I left the ramparts and walked across the main hall where Flavel was discussing what had happened with his officers. When I strode in, he must have seen from my eyes that I intended some mischief. I did not bother about them, I drew my sword and placed it against the rogue's chest. I heard the hiss as his officers also drew their knives and swords. I looked around.

'Messieurs,' I said, 'I do not care what you say or do but one step towards me and I am going to put my sword straight through Monsieur Flavel's throat. Once he is dead, what is the point of you fighting? You are all mercenaries; you would have to account to your masters on why the Maid has been taken and then why you later assassinated someone in her entourage. I suppose,' I said, staring around, 'you already have good explanations for that?'

I looked at their hard faces and blank eyes and knew they would not help Flavel. They were all mercenaries, men who fought for money; they had a certain type of loyalty, but, as long as it did not put their life or limb in extraordinary danger, they would not fight. They returned their swords and daggers to their sheaths, folded their arms and looked at me. I turned back to Flavel; my swordpoint had caught him just above the gorget and I could see a pinprick, a small gem of blood, oozing out of the fleshy part of his throat. Flavel was short, thickset and dark, with eyes close together, so close that his eyebrows seemed to be one long line of hair. He had been a man born in war, made for war, and would probably die there. Although I could see concern in his eyes, I knew he was not frightened. He, too, had reasonably assessed what had happened. The Maid had been taken, I was angry and suspected treason, and if he gave a good enough explanation then the danger would pass. He waited until I had composed myself, making sure that there was no threat from any of his officers. He was a realist; he knew there was very little point in asking them for help. Any plea for mercy would be later used against him as a source of ridicule. So he coolly stared back.

'Monsieur,' he said. 'What is the problem?'

'The problem,' I sardonically replied, 'is that the Maid who led the King's armies in France has been taken by the Burgundians, the allies of England.' I shrugged my shoulders. 'That may be so, she was a soldier and knew the fortunes of war. What I object to is the manner of her taking. Somebody in this city ordered the bells to be rung and so alerted the enemy that the Maid was leaving.' Flavel's eyes slipped away.

'I swear,' he said, 'on my sword hilt that I did not order the bells to be rung.'

I knew he was telling the truth and thought carefully about what he said.

'You may not have ordered the bells to be rung,' I replied. 'But you must know who rang them.'

Flavel shrugged as if it was a matter of little importance.

'We have all sorts of people in the city, Monsieur. They come, they go. It is very easy for someone to slip into the belfry of a church and begin pulling the ropes. After that it is a matter of panic. It is like someone in the crowd shouting "Fire!" You can hardly blame the rest of the crowd for believing it. So it was with this.' I smiled.

'That is very clever, Monsieur Flavel, but you must have found out who started that first bell tolling.' I pressed the sword a little harder and, for the first time, saw genuine alarm and fear in the mercenary captain's eyes.

'Come, Monsieur,' I said slowly. 'It was treachery. The Maid was betrayed. Soon, this year, next year, three or four years hence, someone is going to ask you the same question and your answer must be better than the one you have given me now. Are you going to be proclaimed throughout France as the man who betrayed the Maid?'

I saw fear being replaced by concern in Flavel's eyes as he thought deep and fast.

'I swear,' he muttered, 'I did not order the bells to be rung!'

'But where did it start?' I asked.

'At the church of St. Pierre,' Flavel snapped. 'I have already sent soldiers down there.'

'And?'

Flavel shook his head.

'Nothing. All they found was that a priest had been seen there entering the belfry. The bells sounded within a few minutes. Other church bells took up the sound, believing the city was under attack. You know the rest. By the time the bells had stopped tolling, the Burgundians were alerted and the Maid had been taken.'

'The church of St. Pierre?' I repeated.

Flavel nodded.

'In the Rue Mamoutier.'

'Thank you.' I withdrew my sword, sheathed it and stalked out of the hall.

The church of St. Pierre was a simple building, a long nave with a bell-tower added near the main door. I entered its cool darkness, catching the whiff of incense, sandalwood, resin and spent candle-tallow. The door to the belfry was unlatched so I entered. The ropes hung there in a small chamber, lighted by one window high in the mildewed wall. I looked around at the ropes, long and yellow, snaking down to the floor. I hated them as much as any thinking man can hate a lifeless object; these ropes had trapped the Maid and would send her either to the scaffold or the stake. The dirt floor had been scuffed up. I noticed one imprint, the heelmark of a boot pressed firmly into the packed earth. I bent down to examine it carefully and suddenly realised I was not alone. The hair at the back of my neck curled as if I was some dog. I braced myself for the expected blow, paralysed by fear. I felt the nick of a sharp-pointed sword at the back of my neck and the low voice that I had heard on two previous occasions. The Shadows had returned.

'Well, Master Jankyn,' the voices began. 'So we meet again. We knew you would come here eventually.'

I noticed the word 'we' and tried to turn but the swordpoint pressed deeper into the back of my neck.

'For your own sake, Master Jankyn, do not turn. Listen,' the speaker continued persuasively, though more hurriedly. 'We must leave soon and so must you. Your task is finished.'

'You told me,' I said hoarsely, 'you told me the Maid was safe provided she stayed in Compiegne.'

'Exactly, Jankyn,' the voice replied. 'We knew you would tell the Maid not to leave Compiegne and of course she, being the stubborn bitch she is, would refuse. You see she suspects you, Jankyn. For some strange reason, which we have never understood, she has never handed you over as a traitor or a spy but she did suspect you. Consequently, whatever advice you gave she would act to the contrary. It was a matter of telling you what to say; we knew you would say it and the Maid would leave.'

I felt the blood pound in my head, beating against my temples, and found it difficult to control my breathing.

'You used me!' I replied.

'That is a correct assumption to make,' came the mocking reply. I snarled and began to turn. I felt the blow at the back of my head and slipped into the gathering pool of darkness.

When I awoke it was night, the church still unbolted. My head ached and I felt as if I wanted to vomit. I made my way slowly back through the dark cobbled streets to my lodgings. I managed to obtain some salve and rub it on the large bump at the back of my head. I drank some wine and had a reasonable night's sleep. The next morning I took stock of the situation. The Maid had gone, so my task was finished. In fact, if I stayed here much longer I could well be accused of being both spy and traitor and suffer an ignominious death. The only reasonable thing to do was to return to Beaufort.

One evening I slipped out when a heavy river-mist covered the meadows. I put rags on my horse's hooves and, moving through the heavily wooded countryside, managed to break through the besiegers and made my way west to Rouen. The journey was uneventful enough. I was passing through the war places: deserted villages, devastated farmsteads, the usual picture of carnage and plunder. Those villages which were still inhabited were full of old women and children, the young women in hiding, the men either at war or hidden in the woods. They probably thought I was some Commissioner of Array trying to raise fresh levies for one of the armies ravaging France. I kept myself away from the main thoroughfares, following the river west and concealing myself wherever possible in woods, forests and copses; resting by day and travelling in the late evening or even at night. Eventually I arrived in English-held territory and became more confident and relaxed. I got rid of anything which would link me to the Armagnac faction. I also ensured that my warrants and letters from Beaufort could easily be found and shown to any inquisitive official or soldier.

Ten days after I had left Compiegne, I arrived tired and saddle-sore on the outskirts of Rouen and made my way into the city itself. Rouen has always been a forbidding town. It still bore the scars of Henry's siege some ten years previously; you could see the great oil splashes down the walls where the besiegers had tried to drive off the English. In the city ditch, bones whitened under the autumn sun, lay the skeletons of those whom the defenders had turned out, hoping Henry would let them through his lines on the grounds that they were useless mouths, women and children. Our brave King Henry V, of course, had refused and those useless mouths, penned between the city wall and the besiegers, were allowed to starve.

Inside Rouen there were still areas not yet rebuilt after the fire which had raged in certain quarters. Blackened timber, dust-strewn streets; it may have been the centre of English campaigns in Normandy but it was a depressing, sombre place. Winding cobbled streets, filthy and unpaved; the narrow stone houses crowded together, the corbel beams of one jutting out so far that they almost touched those of the houses at the other side of the street. The place was packed with soldiers; I recognised the ragged bear and staff of Beauchamp, Earl of Warwick, the red and gold tabards of the royal household, and the escutcheons and insignia of at least another ten noble houses. I made enquiries about where Cardinal Beaufort resided and learnt that he, with Warwick and others, were lodged in the castle of Beaurevoir on the other side of Rouen. I stayed in the city, taking lodgings in a small tavern. After a good night's sleep, a proper bath and a change of clothes, I made my way up across the city through the great market-place to the dark, forbidding gatehouse of Beaurevoir Castle.

This was a huge mass of military concrete, large central donjon surrounded by outbuildings, some of stone, some makeshift of wattle and straw, all protected by a high curtain wall which had been strengthened by towers. In one of these towers overlooking the town, Cardinal Beaufort had taken quarters with the young King, Of course, I was not allowed entry immediately. I had to kick my heels for a couple of days until I received a summons from His Satanic Majesty that I should present myself and give an account.

I found Beaufort in a spacious chamber which, as soon as I entered, I knew he had redecorated to suit his own curious tastes. The straw had been removed, the floor cleaned. Thick carpets had been put down and equally costly samite drapes hung on the walls. The room shimmered with gold and silver; a fire burnt in the hearth; the sweetest smelling pine logs had been used and the best furniture in the castle had been moved into the room a large, polished oak table, high-backed chairs, foot-rests, and a huge bolster bed draped with purple, gold-fringed curtains. Braziers, small-grilled, the coals burning red through them, had been placed around the room and the sweetest herbs sprinkled on them to give off a fragrance. You would think you were entering some princess's bedroom rather than that of the chief minister of both church and state.

Beaufort himself, wrapped in a purple cloak, was seated before the fire, his soft-booted feet on a footstool. He stared blankly into the middle distance, a faint smile on his lips as if he was considering some problem, knew the solution, but was still trying to tease his mind with the complexity of what he thought. When I was ushered in he gave me a sidelong glance; his smile broadened and he gestured with the minimum of effort that I should sit opposite him. I noticed he still wore his hands gloved, the fingers decorated with rings studded with the costliest gems and amethysts. I slowly sat down, feeling the soft cushion and luxuriating in the support the great chair gave my back. I realised how rough I had been living these last few months with only benches and stools. I felt a little homesick for the rustic comforts of the widow's house in Orleans, and a little sad and guilty that I had left her without a proper farewell.

I looked at Beaufort, the olive, smooth-skinned face, large dark eyes and petulant mouth. I realised that, despite the smile, the Cardinal was not in the best of humours.

'You have your report, Jankyn?' he began silkily.

'I have, my Lord,' I replied. 'Not written; I prefer to give it verbally because I left Compiegne in some haste and my journey back was not the most easy.'

Beaufort nodded understandingly but his eyes were hard and bleak. He looked at me as if I was some traitor rather than one of his close confidants.

'Master Jankyn,' he continued softly, 'did you serve me well?' I coughed and tried to clear my throat, wondering what was the matter.

'My Lord,' I replied, 'I have always served you well.'

'In this matter, Jankyn?'

'In this matter, my Lord.'

'You were not seduced by the Maid with her subtle strategems and fiendish tricks?'

'My Lord,' I replied, 'the Maid may be an enemy but, in my view, she has nothing to do with Satan.'

Beaufort brought his hand crashing down on the armrest.

'It is for me, Holy Mother Church and the State to decide what the Maid is or may not be. She is a peasant bitch and an Armagnac whore! She has been responsible for the deaths of many Englishmen as well as great defeats. She has set the English cause in France back decades. Only God knows how we will recover.' I was overcome with surprise. I had never seen Beaufort so angry. His eyes blazed and even when he had finished speaking his mouth moved wordlessly as if giving vent to some great hatred.

At last, he composed himself. 'All right, Jankyn,' he said, with his eyes measuring me as if I was already guilty but he was deciding to postpone my punishment for some future occasion, 'you had better give me your report.'

It must have been mid-morning when I began and I continued late into the afternoon. Outside, it fell dark and a mist began to seep in through the cracks in the horn-glazed windows, spreading a chill in the room. Beaufort ordered fresh logs to be put on the fire, the braziers to be wheeled near, and mulled wine and hot meats to be brought for the sustenance of us both. He rarely interrupted me, but let me speak as I gave him a factual report of what had happened. I say factual, not truthful. I had sensed the Cardinal's mood. I began to tell him what he wanted to hear rather than what I would have liked to have said. Beaufort heard me out, listening to me carefully but now and again throwing me the odd shrewd glance as if he could read my mind. Sometimes, when he did interrupt, he would ask me to repeat certain passages, particularly whenever I

touched upon the Maid's links with her voices or claims
that she was sent by God. I also sensed that Beaufort was
not only angry but frightened and I found this strange,
for if the Cardinal was anything he was courageous. He
feared no man, but I cannot really say whether he
feared God.

I believe he memorised every word and every nuance
of my speech. It was evening before we finished.
Afterwards he sat for what must have been almost an
hour, acting as if I was not there. He just stared into the
fire, his purple-gloved fingers drumming gently on the
arm of the chair. At last he looked up and smiled
wearily.

'It is good to see you, Jankyn,' he said softly. 'You did
more perhaps than I expected. Do you have any
questions?'

'The Shadows,' I said. Beaufort looked puzzled. 'The
men who came to see me,' I continued. 'Who were
always in the dark. Who were they?'

Beaufort bit his lower lip and smiled as if savouring
some secret joke.

'I knew of them but I did not send them,' he said.
'Perhaps, one day, you will meet the Shadows.'

'I hope so,' I interjected grimly. 'I have scores to settle
with them!'

'Not now, not now, Jankyn,' Beaufort said smoothly.
'For the moment, we must finish this business.'

'How?' I asked.

Beaufort looked at me strangely. 'You know there is
only one way, Jankyn.'

'There could be others.'

Beaufort moved his mouth and shrugged. 'Perhaps,'
he said.

He suddenly stirred himself. 'Look. Take some sleep
and come back to me.' He extended a hand. I rose, went
on one knee and kissed the jewels on his fingers. He
patted me gently on the head as if I was some faithful

dog. 'Go now, Jankyn.'

I left, looking back once to see Beaufort, head cradled in one hand, staring bleakly into the fire.

# FOURTEEN

The next morning, I presented myself in the Cardinal's chamber. I found him more businesslike though still wrapped in his great purple robe against the cold which he complained about constantly. He seemed more aggressive, keener to continue the business in hand. Whereas the day before he had been silent, now he displayed his ruthlessness in a series of stark, blunt questions. He began:

'What do you think of the Maid?'

'What do I think?' I replied testily. 'I think she is an exceptional person.'

'You know what I mean,' Beaufort interjected. 'Where does she come from? Heaven or Hell?'

'I do not know,' I replied honestly. 'All I know is what I saw and what I told you yesterday. She is a young girl with exceptional qualities.'

Beaufort laughed and clapped me on the shoulder. 'That is what I like about you, Jankyn. Your feet are firmly planted in this world. You haven't even got half an eye on the next.'

'What do you think, my Lord?' I asked. 'Is she from God?'

Beaufort bit his lip. 'Look, Jankyn, we live in dangerous times. England has a sickly young king, a young man who so far in his nine years has not displayed the iron nature and steel hand he will need to control this kingdom. Can you imagine, Jankyn, what it

would be like if France became united? A great power
stretching from the northern provinces down to the
mountains of Italy and Spain. You have seen the
countryside. Admittedly it is devastated by war, but can
you imagine it in peace? What chance would England
have then against all these resources, the wealth and the
manpower and its great fleets patrolling the Channel
and the seas on either side of England? Look, it is only
forty years ago that this same nation sent its fleet to
burn all the towns on our southern coast – in our
lifetime, Jankyn. For God's sake, it may happen again!'
Beaufort stopped as if surprised by his own vehemence.
He continued, 'I am a man of the Church yet our
Church is under attack from within its own ranks and by
heretics within. There are stirrings with men wishing to
throw off the Church's authority and deny her
obedience. What would happen, Jankyn? Every man
thinking himself an authority on sacred scripture and
being prepared to pontificate on divine truths? I
represent order, Jankyn. Order in Church and State. If
that goes, the devastation in France will be nothing
compared to what will happen.'

Beaufort was being honest because he was worried
and frightened, so honesty was also my best venture.

'My Lord,' I replied, 'what has that got to do with the
Maid?'

'Everything!' Beaufort replied. 'She attacks the
authority of the Church. She claims divine intervention.
She believes Heaven speaks to her directly. What
happens if everybody believed that? She has led the
Dauphin's armies and brought them to victory. If
England withdraws from France because of her, it will
be seen as God's judgement and so what would happen
to England? Shall we, in ten or twenty years' time, face
another Duke William from Normandy, another
French general wishing to devastate the southern shires
of England?'

'But what if the Maid *is* sent from Heaven?' I persisted. 'How do we know that?' Beaufort replied. 'What is Heaven's will? France is full of visionaries. Do you know that Regnault, Archibishop of Rheims, now has a new shepherd-boy who claims that he has been sent by God and denounces Jehanne as an imposter and trickster? So what is God's will? If God wills anything, he must have willed the victory at Agincourt.'

'Perhaps God has changed his mind,' I added jestingly. Beaufort bit his lip which was a sign that he was agitated. He rose from his chair and walked restlessly up and down the room.

'We do not know the Maid has been sent by Heaven,' Beaufort replied. He then continued softly, 'But again you see, Jankyn, if we accept that she has then we must leave France. Once we have left, how do we know that in England, itself, we may not have visionaries claiming we are supposed to do this or supposed to do that? I am a man of the Church, Jankyn, but I live in the world. I must be guided by what happens here, by what I can see and what I can feel.' Beaufort continued bitingly, 'Moreover, if God had ordained that the Maid be sent by Him, why has He delivered her into our hands? Why has she failed to take Paris? Why did she fail to relieve Compiegne?'

'She has,' I pointed out. 'Compiegne has since been relieved.'

Beaufort snorted and turned away. 'Let us accept, Jankyn, for the sake of argument, that there is some practical, ordinary explanation for what happened. Tell me how you would explain it in natural, rational terms.'

I had expected this question and had my own answer ready.

'My Lord,' I said. 'Firstly, France is full of visionaries, women who prophesy how one day the English will leave France. Consequently, the Maid emerged to a people already prepared for her message.'

Beaufort nodded. 'Go on,' he said.

'Then,' I said, 'there are the Maid's origins. She was regarded as something special by her own family. Jehanne said she heard the voices of St. Catherine, St. Michael and St. Margaret. Is is not a coincidence that in her neighbourhood there is a statue dedicated to St. Margaret, which is in her chapel at Domremy, as well as churches dedicated to St. Michael and St. Catherine? They almost form a triangle around her house.' I continued slowly: 'There again, she says that the voices began to speak to her when the bells of those churches sounded. Is it possible that she thought the bells were the voices of her saints? I mean, there is a fairground trick where someone can put another person in a trance at the mention of a certain word and have them do what they wish. I have seen it many a time and you, my Lord, must have heard of it.' Beaufort nodded. 'Perhaps,' I shrugged, 'this could be the case with the Maid.'

'But her victories?' Beaufort persisted. 'How do you explain them, and her acceptance by the Dauphin?'

'My Lord,' I answered, 'what do you fear most? What are you ashamed of most?' Beaufort looked at me strangely but I persisted. 'You are, and I say this without insult, my Lord, a member of a house which is a bastard line of a king.' I saw the colour deepen in Beaufort's face. 'Look,' I cried, 'your face betrays you. Despite being a Bishop and Cardinal of the Church, you still feel this deeply.'

'What has that got to do with the Dauphin?' Beaufort said peevishly.

'It has everything to do with him,' I replied. 'For years the Dauphin was proclaimed as a bastard. His own mother announced he might be illegitimate. It was his great fear. Now a Maid, a prophetess sent by God, comes to Court proclaiming he is of legitimate blood and the true heir to the French crown. She claims that she brings this message direct from Heaven.' I continued smoothly, 'I ask you humbly, my Lord, what

would your reaction be if someone, claiming to come
from God, arrived at Westminster with the news that
you were not of a bastard issue but of the true line of the
crown of England?'

Beaufort stood still, looking at me sideways. 'Go on,'
he said softly.

'Again, the victories,' I said.

'What victories?'

'Orleans was besieged by a force too inferior to take it
and by a commander too incompetent. With all due
respect, my Lord, we know the Lord Suffolk is a good
man but if Salisbury had been there who knows what
might have been. Again, Patay. I was there, my Lord. A
succession of incompetent blunders by our forces. The
English generals were divided. It is well known that
Talbot is against Falstaff and Falstaff is against Talbot;
they led an inferior force, fighting in terrain they did
not know, against an enemy which knew the land well.' I
continued hastily, 'Moreover, the French are well led.
They have good generals. They have learnt the lessons
of Agincourt. D'Alençon, the Bastard of Orleans, and
La Hire are probably the best generals the French have.
And why not?' I asked, rising from my chair, now
excited by the vehemence of my own words. 'This is not
the first time the French have defeated us. Fifty years
ago, they defeated us under the Gascon, Bertrand de
Guesclin. Nobody claimed he was sent by God. He was a
thickset, poxy, wily Gascon who applied the same tactics
and drove us out. If you look at our affairs then, it was a
similar situation, with a divided English command and a
weak ruler at home. What is so different now?' I added
honestly, 'Remember, the Maid had her defeats. She
was captured at Compiegne, lost Soissons and was
driven off Paris. What else is there to say?'

Beaufort slumped into a chair with his fingers
drumming restlessly on the table-top. 'And the future?'
he said. 'What about that, Jankyn?'

'What about it?' I replied. 'Look, my Lord, the Maid has been deserted by Charles of France. She has been defeated in battle and captured by her enemies. Has Charles lifted one finger to help her? No, he has not. Has he made any attempt to either rescue or ransom her? No, he has not. Why not hold her for a while, interrogate her, challenge her to make peace and eventually let her go? Then she will be nothing. We would see her as something so ridiculous as not to be worthy of our attention.'

'And the French?'

I shrugged. 'They could draw their own conclusions.'

Beaufort looked at me strangely. 'But if we let her go,' he said, 'we are part of her heresy.'

'No,' I said. 'We simply ignore her for what she is.' I looked at him steadily, hiding my lies. 'We turn her from our Court as a fool, a peasant not worthy of our attention.'

Beaufort shook his head. 'We cannot do that,' he said. 'The blood of Patay, of Orleans and those she has killed in battle cries to Heaven for vengeance.' Lifting a finger, he added, 'But what happens if we let her escape, Jankyn?'

I looked at him and smiled. For the first time since I had met him I felt some stirring of affection for this sleek, cunning, most sly of priests. I bowed and left with Beaufort's words ringing like some melody in my head.

During the next few weeks I stayed around Rouen attempting to be busy but all the time keeping a sharp watch on what was happening to the Maid elsewhere. I really surprised myself. I usually care for nobody. I still don't. In my life I have been many things, but not a hypocrite. I have never supported noble causes. I hate those empty men who, with clever words and high-sounding phrases, adopt lofty ideals and so delude themselves.

I could have left Rouen for England. Beaufort never

insisted that I stayed. He had made it quite clear my service to him was ended by paying me a large gift of gold, anonymously and quietly, with all the care and courtesy of which he was capable. I thought of my manor in Newport with its fresh, green fields, the even pace of its day. I felt homesick and wanted to return but I also wanted to see the matter through. I watched, like some open-mouthed peasant, as the drama of the Maid unfolded before me.

Jehanne had been held in a number of fortresses before eventually being moved to the castle of Beaulieu, near Noyon. I knew of it. An impressive fortress surrounded by dark, melancholy forests. Octagonal in plan it was a huge, circular donjon fifty feet high protected by a deep moat. The Maid was alone, except for Delon. I felt a stirring of sympathy, for only then did I remember that Delon had been taken with his mistress.

At first, the Count of Luxembourg (her real captor, since his retainers had taken her) treated Jehanne with honour and care. The Maid was in good spirits, believing her capture was only a temporary setback and that she would be allowed to escape. While she was at Beaulieu, she made the first attempt. The room where she was kept had a planked floor. She prised part of this up, got into a lower room, and was just about to lock the guards in their own guardroom when she was surprised by a porter. From then on, the Maid was kept in a small, dark cell for she insisted she would escape if she saw the chance. Her attempt, coupled with a defiant attitude, made Luxembourg transfer her to another huge, sombre fortress, also in the middle of dense forests, far enough away from the Armagnac lines to prevent any attempt by the Maid to escape. Here, she was treated well and struck up a cordial relationship with Jeanne de Luxembourg, the Count's wife. The latter attempted to persuade Jehanne to wear women's clothes by offering her some cloth to make them, but the Maid refused to comply, saying she would only do so at God's commandment.

I also learnt about the reaction to the Maid's capture. In the Armagnac quarters of Orleans, Tours and Blois, there had been public prayers and general processions in which the clergy had walked barefoot through the towns beseeching God to deliver the Maid. Perhaps the most sinister and depressing aspect had been the reaction of Charles and his ministers. Regnault, Archbishop of Rheims, the same who had stood beside the Maid when Charles was crowned, had written to his people telling them what had happened to the Maid. He dismissed her as a trickster and pretender and commended his own miracle worker. This was the person I have mentioned earlier, the young shepherd from the mountains who had now taken God's command to accompany Charles' troops. Silly bastards all!

I suppose if the Maid had heard of this it would have been enough to drive her, or any person, to suicide. Here was the King's own minister and principal archbishop dismissing her as a trickster. Within days of her capture, he was ready to replace her with some peasant boy who also claimed to be a visionary. A nasty, pernicious bastard, Regnault of Rheims, who, together with La Tremoille, made sure King Charles did nothing. Oh, I know I am an old man now! I know when Charles entered Rouen some twenty years later, he ordered an investigation into what had happened. Stupid sod! What is the use of investigations when the tragedy has happened and someone has been disgraced? Charles deserted Jehanne. Not one penny did he raise for ransom or send one soldier to free her or one envoy to treat with Bedford or Burgundy. Strange isn't it – years later, when the King became infatuated with his mistress, Agnes Sorel, whatever she asked he did. But for the Maid, who delivered a kingdom to him, he did nothing and nor did any of his captains. I, a rogue amongst rogues, always thought I could fall no lower. As always, I am wrong. I have seen Charles and his generals and their treatment of the Maid. Bastards all; under the sun there are worse than me. Whenever I study the Good Book (at night, just in case I die in my sleep) and read the words of the psalmist, 'Oh, put not your trust in princes', I accept that the man who wrote them was a prophet, who foresaw the shambling, weak-kneed monkey of a man known in history as Charles VII of France.

In Rouen, as I said, I hung around the castle carrying out tasks for Beaufort and taking messages to the hawk-nosed, blond-haired Bedford. Pompous and fat-faced, he was able and efficient and ruled France in young Henry's name. He hated Beaufort almost as much as Beaufort hated him. Bedford's wife, however, I found to be a pleasant-faced, lumpy sort of woman. She was Burgundy's sister and Bedford had married her to cement the alliance between the two factions. She, at least, was kind and when she heard I had served with the Maid, often used to question me about her. I gave her truthful answers. She said she would do something, but with her hands which fluttered in front of her face, her white, dough-like skin and large cow-eyes, I really wondered how effective she would be. The third member of the unholy trinity was Beauchamp, Earl of Warwick. He seemed to have two natures in the one body. Chivalrous and courteous, he could also be as cruel as a scavenging wolf or merciless as a hawk in its death flight. These three men stayed in Rouen and plotted against the Maid.

She was still held in Luxembourg and negotiations were going on to see who would buy her. Would it be Burgundy or England? Jehanne had tried to escape again by throwing herself off a seventy-foot-high tower, claiming God had directed her to rejoin the French to fight against the invaders. Only God knows how she survived such a fall. She was picked up dazed and confused but had hardly suffered any injury whatsover. When Beaufort heard about this incident, he seemed satisfied. This was proof that the Maid had some sort of satanic power; every self-respecting witch or warlock claimed they could fly.

'Perhaps,' he mused, 'Jehanne was trying to prove this.'

'That is ridiculous,' I retorted. 'The Maid has been deserted by her own King and his Court. Maybe she is susceptible to other human feelings, even humours and vapours. Perhaps she just panicked.'

Beaufort looked at me sideways.

'Perhaps,' he said. 'We will have to see.'

Well, that's enough for now. I am tired and I'm crying. This little turd of a priest who's copying my words is looking at me strangely. What does he know? I've heard him mutter the Maid was a witch. Only the Sweet Jesus knows the truth. All I remember are her sad grey eyes as she was hunted. For being a witch? For being a peasant, for being French and, above all, for being a woman who thrashed the generals England could field. Who cares? I'm growing maudlin and a bottle of sack is the best cure for that. Tomorrow I'll continue about Jehanne. Sweet Christ, I just liked her.

# FIFTEEN

I should not have feared Beaufort, for a new and more sinister bastard had now come upon the scene. He was Pierre Cauchon, Bishop of Beauvais. An intelligent and energetic man, Cauchon's talents were only matched by his lack of moderation. He had a will as formidable as that of the Maid as well as a vindictive, vicious streak in his nature which she would certainly feel. He was well-named. Cauchon is remarkably similar to the French word for pig. From the start, Cauchon had been with the Armagnac cause, associating with the members of the University of Paris who were already writing letters demanding the Maid be surrendered either to England or the Church to receive her just rewards. In Paris, he had proceeded from responsibility to responsibility for he had a brilliant, keen intellect. An expert in law, he had been elected to the See of Beauvais in 1420. However, Cauchon and the rest of his friends were driven from the bishopric when the Maid appeared. He had fled to Rouen where he had spent most of his time reflecting on the wrongs he had suffered and the indignity which had been heaped upon him as the result of the triumphal campaigns of the idolatrous, sorceress Maid.

Cauchon had the reputation of being a man who never forgot and never forgave. This coldly revengeful prelate now took over the task assigned to him by Bedford and Beaufort of collecting evidence against the

Maid and empanelling a Church court to try her for treason, heresy and witchcraft. He flitted like some great bat from camp to camp, castle to castle and town to town. He visited Jean of Luxembourg and demanded, in the name of the Church, King Henry VI and the University of Paris, that the Maid be surrendered to him for, according to canon law, he should try her for witchcraft as she had been captured in his diocese.

Bishop Pig returned to Rouen to confer with Bedford, Warwick and Beaufort. As you will realise, I met him there. Cauchon was a large, florid-faced man with slate-blue eyes and vice-like mouth. He was a man who could be charming and tactful but, when hindered or blocked, displayed a vicious streak which even a rat would have despaired of. All the time, he spun his greasy web, his one aim being to bring the Maid into his power and to have her tried. He was aided and abetted by two imps from hell: one, a canon called Loiselleur and the other, a notary called D'Estivez. I met them once in a corridor. They passed me by without a glance but I could smell the wickedness exuding from them. Dressed in black, each of them had pinched features, hard eyes and thin, prim lips. They were the sort of men who would send their mothers to the stake in the name of the good Christ or the common good. These lawyers had massive sums placed at their disposal as they negotiated and bargained for Jehanne with both Burgundy and Luxembourg. Burgundy had a say because the Maid was fighting his troops when she was captured and Luxembourg was, technically, Burgundy's vassal.

There was little I could do but watch and listen as the tragic pageant unfolded. The Maid, after her second attempted escape, was moved to Arras, then to le Crotoy on the sea at the mouth of the Somme before being finally moved south-east to Rouen. She arrived during a slashing rainstorm on the day before Christmas Eve and was quietly brought in, guarded by a ring of men-at-arms. I could not watch for I was too ashamed. Like Judas, I concealed myself in one of the outhouses and watched the riders splash through the muddy courtyard and dismount. I caught a glimpse of the Maid dressed in the dark jerkin and leggings of a squire. Her hair was still cropped short and her face pale, pinched and white. She was taken up into the Tour de Tresor near the back gate of the castle, which overlooked the fields. Built by Philip Augustus to house royal monies, it proved to be an excellent prison for the Maid. She was put on the first floor, up a flight of steps near the castle chapel, and given a room with a bed and chair, but they insisted on padlocking her with a great chain around her middle. The chain was attached to a wooden beam and, although it allowed her to walk and sit down, her movements were confined.

Five English soldiers were appointed to guard her day and night in the cell. They were under a master bowman called John Grey but they were not the best of gaolers for soldiers are superstitious men and what they fear they taunt and attack. The cell door was heavily padlocked with one key being given to the Vice-Inquisitor of Paris who had been summoned by Cauchon to join him for the trial. Another key was given to the Earl of Warwick and the last one to Cardinal Beaufort, Bishop of Winchester. I complained to Beaufort about the limitations of Jehanne's quarters saying it would reflect badly on him and others if the Maid was treated with any vindictiveness before her trial. Beaufort just smiled and shrugged.

'She should count herself lucky, Master Jankyn,' he replied. 'If Cauchon had his way, he would place her in an iron cage and fasten her by the neck, hands and feet. The only reason she is not there is because of my intervention. Leave her well alone!' He looked at me sharply. 'You have visited her?'

'Not yet,' I replied.

'You may when you wish,' Beaufort taunted. He knew full well that I felt embarrassed about visiting someone in prison who had last seen me as a friend and would now regard me as a traitor.

Other people did visit her. Beaufort, the Earl of Stafford who was also residing in Rouen, Warwick and Bedford all went to interrogate her. At one point, Bedford remonstrated with her over her past victories. The Maid, impetuous as ever, replied that even if there were a hundred thousand Goddamns in France, the kingdom would eventually be free of them and returned to its rightful ruler. At this, Stafford was so incensed that he drew his sword and attempted to stab her and was only prevented from doing so by the Earl of Warwick.

Nevertheless, the Maid's real enemies were not Warwick, Stafford and Beauford, but Cauchon and his coven. He now had them assembled. One was Jean Massieu who was a cheery-faced, black-haired little man who would act as tipstaff. I got to know him well by deliberately cultivating his company, whenever possible buying him drinks in the taverns around the castle. Massieu was sympathetic towards the Maid. He was a compassionate man and the only member of Cauchon's panel I found to be approachable. As for the rest, well in my view they were rats on a garbage heap. They were Thomas de Courcelles, a brilliant lawyer who hid his pride behind false humility, the clerk, Manchon, and the assessor, Nicholas Midi. They were men full of sanctity as well as their own importance. There was also Jean Beaupere who had lost one of his hands to brigands while travelling between Beauvais and Paris. Finally, the two greatest shits of them all, Jean D'Estivez, the promoter of the cause, and Loiselleur.

The Christmas season passed, muted and sombre

because of the prisoner in the castle. There were the usual yuletide celebrations with the boy bishop and the master serving the servants. Tumblers, actors and fire-eaters were all invited to the castle to enliven the company of the great. A shaggy bear was brought in to be baited by the castle dogs but, after he had killed four of them, he was led away. Everyone knew that the real spectacle, the real drama, was contained in the Tour de Tresor and they were waiting for the actors to take their places on the stage.

The month of January was cold, hard, with biting blizzards, and the ground was covered in thick, black ice. I had been given quarters very near to those of Beaufort and I rarely left them. Sometimes, I just sat thinking about my life, wondering about the Maid and feeling guilty about what I had done. You see, I have very little conscience but, when it is pricked, it hurts. It hurts terribly. I heard what they were doing to the Maid, the baiting of the soldiers who, whilst they never actually raped her, constantly taunted her with the prospect. But what made me sick was the behaviour of Loiselleur. He was put in the same cell as the Maid and, pretending to be her friend, tried to draw her into treasonable conversation. After that, he sent a priest in to hear her confession, but what the Maid did not know was that Loiselleur and others hid in a secret chamber behind the Maid's cell to watch and listen to what went on. This callous cruelty prompted me to act. I approached the Tour de Tresor, making my way across the backyard and up the steps. I knocked on the door but was not allowed access. To obtain that I would need to have the permission of all three key-holders. But I thought I might be able to speak through the grille. An English archer pushed his ugly, bulbous-nosed face against the door and peered out.

'What do you wish, clerk?' he asked.

'I am here on behalf of Lord Beaufort, Bishop of

Winchester and Cardinal of England. I wish a word with the Maid.'

The archer looked at me suspiciously. 'Do you have permission?'

'Do you want me to go back and get it?' I taunted. 'You can always do it yourself. You will find I am of the household of Bishop Beaufort and I have a close interest in this matter.'

The archer retorted by belching in my face. 'How many people have an interest in this case?' He turned and not waiting for an answer yelled, 'Hey you, whore, come here!' I heard the clank of chains and the slow slither of footsteps across the straw-packed floor, then the Maid's face was up against the grille. I expected a stream of profanities, spittle and abuse, but when she saw me she smiled, her eyes crinkling. I felt profoundly sorry for her, with her black, cropped hair and pale, pinched face. She was like some small animal brought to bay yet she could still summon up a smile.

'So, Jankyn,' she said softly, 'I was right. You are a spy.' Almost conversationally, as if we had met the previous day, she carried on, 'You know, I often said to Delon, but there is some goodness in your heart. I have seen it there.' She grinned and then her face became serious as tears filled her eyes. 'Surely, however, you have not come to taunt me? Not you.'

I replied hoarsely, almost whispering, although the archer had moved away. I suppose, like his kind, he had his own code and eavesdropping was not part of it. 'Madame, madame, yes I was a spy sent into your camp but I swear, on the Sacrament, that I had nothing to do with your capture!'

The Maid nodded. 'I know that,' she replied. 'So what are you doing here?'

'Listen,' I said. 'You may still escape.' God forbid, but I saw the hope flame into her eyes like a sudden fire which blazes up when oil has been poured on it. I continued hoarsely, 'I do not know how or when, but until the trial I pray and beg you to beware of Loiselleur!'

She looked at me strangely.

'The priest,' I said. 'He is an actor. He is still a priest but one in the pay of the English. Take care how you treat him.'

The Maid nodded and lowered her face so I could not see the tears falling down her cheeks. Here was another betrayal. Jehanne looked sharply up at me.

'What will they do, Jankyn?'

I shook my head wordlessly.

'Take courage!' I said.

The Maid smiled and moved away. The grille slammed fast in my face.

I was too aggrieved in spirit and too depressed with the evil humours of the prison to go back to my garret so I wandered out of the castle down into the streets of Rouen. I passed the devastated quarters with the houses no more than a collection of charred timbers. Rows and rows of poor people with men missing a leg, a hand, an arm or an eye, all because of the war. Widows with orphans, their menfolk killed, thronged the market-place beseeching alms and asking for help. I looked at them, listened to the cries, saw the dirt and the filth. For a few seconds I knew what Christ must have felt as He, the Holy One, moved through the filth and dirt in Jerusalem. I also saw, in a way, why the Maid was necessary. If I was God, I would have certainly raised up someone to end the war. What confused me was why He hadn't finished the task and allowed the Maid complete victory.

I returned to the castle and bluntly asked for an audience with Beaufort. Of course he refused, and told me to return the following morning. When I did, I found him behind his great oaken desk busily sealing documents and snapping sharply at some poor clerk. I could see that he was not in the best of moods so I sat and waited until he had finished, dismissing the clerk with a cursory nod of his head.

'Well, Jankyn,' he asked, stretching his arms to ease the cramp after so much writing. 'What is the problem?'

'The problem, my Lord,' I replied, 'is the Maid.'

'Yes,' Beaufort said sarcastically. 'I know the problem but what can I do?'

'It is the future, my Lord. The Maid will be brought to trial?' Beaufort nodded. 'Found guilty?' Beaufort nodded. 'And handed over to the secular arm for punishment?' Beaufort nodded again. I realised he was gently ridiculing me.

'That is obvious, Jankyn.'

'And she will be burnt?'

'Probably.'

I felt my blood turn as cold as the sleet which was hammering on the horned-glassed window. 'She will be killed.'

'Yes, yes,' Beaufort replied testily. 'She will be killed! She will receive her just merits for the crimes she has committed.'

'And you will make her a martyr for France?' Beaufort stopped fidgeting and looked narrowly at me. 'Oh come, my Lord,' I said, taking my turn to be sarcastic, 'you must have thought of that! Someone dead can be more powerful than someone alive. We both have seen it happen before. Richard II of England. He was a despot, a tyrant, unsupported, unloved, but he incited more revolts, conspiracies and dissensions after his deposition and imprisonment than he ever caused during his life.'

'You are saying that the Maid,' Beaufort continued slowly, 'could do that in France?'

'Perhaps,' I said. ' "The Goddamns have killed a saint!" You can hear the cry echoing from town to town.' I now had Beaufort's attention. He turned so that he sat squarely facing me. 'Surely, my Lord,' I repeated, 'you have thought of this?'

'Yes, I have,' Beaufort replied. 'It sounds more threatening coming from you. Go on. Proceed with what you are saying.'

I shrugged. 'It is quite simple. You are giving the Dauphin and the French a martyr for their cause.' I dealt my argument a final twist. 'Who knows, perhaps that is what La Tremoille wants. On the one hand, he gains a martyr for his cause, and, on the other, we arrange for a nuisance to be removed.'

'But,' Beaufort interrupted, 'if we do not remove her, we do not do justice to the defeats we have sustained, the casualties and the terrible wrongs she has inflicted upon us.'

'But, my Lord,' I replied. 'Need we kill her? We could imprison her, even allow her to escape or pretend someone dies in her stead to create confusion, doubt and uncertainty.'

Beaufort nodded and waved a beringed hand at me. 'I will think about what you have said, Jankyn. I will ask you to return to repeat your sentiments in front of someone else.'

A few days later, Beaufort sent for me again. I remember it was the end of January. Already the secret interrogation of the Maid had begun, with Cauchon and others visiting her in her cell asking questions, probing and trying to entrap her. I entered Beaufort's chamber expecting to find him by himself but Cauchon, Lord Pigface, sat with him at the corner of the great oak table. Cauchon, wrapped in a blue, fur-adorned robe, glared at me as if I was his enemy even though he had never spoken to me in his life. Beside him, dressed in a brown robe and hood with a face like a bull mastiff with blue, watery eyes, was the Vice-Inquisitor for France, a man with a terrible reputation but without the strength of character or force of will to match. He looked at me nervously, licked his lips and carefully studied the design on one of Beaufort's carpets.

It must have been late in the afternoon because the beautiful white candles in the candelabra around the room had been lit. I will always remember the cloying warmth and faint scent of perfume contrasting so starkly with Cauchon's threatening presence. Beaufort greeted me solicitously, ushering me to a seat and assuring Bishop Pig that I was one of his agents who had been responsible for the Maid falling into their hands. Cauchon seemed to dismiss this. He just smirked and continued to play with a large purple amethyst on the finger of his left hand.

'Master Jankyn,' Beaufort began quietly, 'has a few thoughts about our prisoner in the tower.' He turned to me and nodded so I gave Cauchon the same explanation, tempered, but more hard and powerful than the argument I had given Beaufort. Cauchon sat and heard me out, leaning forward to miss nothing. I, however, even though I was used to danger, recoiled from the glittering hatred in his eyes.

'The Maid,' he replied, 'is an apostate, a heretic, a traitor and a sorceress. She deserves to die.'

I felt my temper rise and wanted to smash my fist straight into his fat, podgy, arrogant face but I controlled myself.

'I accept, my Lord,' I said, 'all you have said, but would the Maid's death achieve everything you want?'

'Justice!' the Bishop shouted.

I will tell you this. People who cry for justice, especially when they are fat and hold high office, are usually dangerous people and are not to be trusted. You will not find this opinion in any book or manuscript of political theories or maxims. It is truth acquired from hard observation, and it certainly applied to Cauchon. He did not want justice but revenge. Revenge for losing his town, revenge for losing his diocese, and revenge on a woman who had usurped his place in society. I could see Jehanne was lost. I rose, bowed to Beaufort and stalked out of the room ignoring his shouts for me to return.

That night I drank myself stupid on the raw, red wine served out to the castle garrison. I was so incapable I could hardly stand, and I flopped about shouting that Beaufort was a bastard and the Maid should be freed. My voice rang through the castle yard. God knows what mischief I might have incurred if some friendly guard, tired of my rantings, had not hit me unconscious on the back of the head with an empty wine bottle. The following morning, I woke shivering in the freezing cold in one of the outhouses of the castle yard. A large dog came up, sniffed me before urinating over one of my legs. This act of contempt by a mere animal forced me to rise and I staggered back to my own quarters where I bathed, changed and fell into a deep sleep. When I awoke, I managed to scrounge food from the kitchen, some hot soup and watered ale. This satisfied my ravenous appetite whilst I tried to remember if I had said something which could put me in any danger. I still cursed Cauchon's arrogant attitude and the deep hatred in the castle towards the Maid. I was, therefore, surprised when the door opened and Beaufort slipped in, wrapped in a thick black cloak with the hood pulled forward. He sat on my garret's only stool and pushed his hood back. He stared at me in that concerned, false manner one expects of a physician expecting a good fee.

'My Lord,' I mumbled, trying to regain my wits, 'I am honoured.'

'How could I ignore such an occasion?' Beaufort interrupted drily. 'You are ill?'

'I was drunk,' I replied.

'So you were, Jankyn,' Beaufort commented. 'I heard your shouting as did the whole garrison. The only person who didn't, thank God, was the Duke of

Bedford, otherwise he might have had your head.' I apologised as humbly as I could but Beaufort pushed my apologies aside. 'You hate Cauchon?'

'I hate his stupidity, his arrogance and his venom,' I replied. 'I am a coward, my Lord, you know that. But I know what I have seen.' I continued suddenly, 'What if ... what if the Maid was sent from God? Do you wish a saint's blood on your hands?'

Beaufort shrugged. 'In this war with France, many innocents have died. Young children, mothers and babes in arms. It is a fact of our existence,' he replied. 'Just as I accept that there may be assassins, here in Rouen, who would be only too happy to plant a crossbow bolt between my shoulder-blades or sink a dagger under my ribs, the Maid knew the dangers which faced her. She accepted them. I cannot speak for God but only for the duty entrusted to me.' Beaufort continued as if to stop the argument: 'However, I have thought about what you said.' He leaned forward and, with the hem of his robe, wiped a bit of slush from one of his black, Spanish leather boots. 'I believe you are correct, Jankyn. The Maid must be persuaded to recant, to abjure. If she does that then she can have her life and maybe even her freedom.' He held up his hand. 'For the moment, leave the matter. When the time is ripe, we shall talk again.'

# SIXTEEN

Over the next few weeks, I thought about what Beaufort had disclosed of his real intentions. He kept his distance from me as the great ones in the castle began to plot the Maid's destruction. Cauchon and his assessors visited her in her cell every day. From the chatter and the gossip around the castle, the Maid gave good, sharp, tart replies thereby successfully eluding any attempt to trap her. Her interrogators were following the rules of the Inquisition but Jehanne was able to take care of such questions. She adroitly answered them, strong in her belief that she had been sent from God. To be quite honest (and I can see the priest who is transcribing this for me beginning to wince because he believes I am an evil old man) I am not too sure whether my feelings about the Maid are because of the buxom wench lying beside me to keep me warm, or because of what I believe about her. Well, who cares? The priest is a cretinous bastard who does not understand what it is like to be caught up amongst the great ones of this world. I must remember to beat him soundly.

Anyway, I digress. I really couldn't have cared whether the Maid was sent from God or by the Lord Pope. All I knew was the loyalty I felt for her. Above all, I hated Cauchon and the snarling pack which surrounded her, snapping at her. They were people who on the field of battle (and I speak as a professional coward) would not dare to meet her lance for lance or sword for sword but now she was chained to a beam could taunt and bait her.

At last they brought her to trial, with the first session taking place on Wednesday, 21st March, 1431. The Maid was led by an armed escort from her chamber into the Chapel Royal which stood in the middle of the castle courtyard. Cauchon and his team of assessors awaited her. I didn't attend. I hated Cauchon's pig-face so much I would have openly attacked him, exposing him for what he was, a liar. He sat there, so I understand, on his canopied throne like a great, fat spider. All around him was the visible power of the Church and State aiding and abetting him in the lies he spun to trap a nineteen-year-old peasant girl who was fighting for her life. Manchon, one of the clerks I cultivated as a matter of course, told me what happened. He said that at the first interrogation, indeed at the first question, a vicious tumult arose, with Jehanne being interrupted at every word. So great that he complained, and declared that if things were not more orderly he would not accept the responsibility of drawing up a correct report of the meeting.

The real struggle took place with Jehanne's refusal to take the oath. When she was asked to tell the truth, the Maid replied:

'I do not know what you will ask me about. Perhaps you will ask me things which I shall not tell you.' She made it quite clear she would not reveal her revelations to Charles VII. Consequently, she took a strictly limited oath, saying that as long as she was not asked certain questions she would give honest answers. Cauchon tried to trap her by asking her to say the 'Our Father' which is a well-known trick, for wizards, warlocks and sorceresses are unable to recite it. The Maid gaily answered that she would say it on the condition that he would hear her confession. This caused a low murmur of laughter in the room and Lord Pig-Face angrily forbade the Maid to make fun of him.

Oh, by the way, I know there is an account of Jehanne's trial. Don't believe everything it says. Cauchon kept it to himself for months before publishing his own edited version. Many of the clerks and notaries there, even though they were in the pay of either Burgundy or England, bitterly complained at having to write out everything the Maid said. They all knew Cauchon would later edit their minutes to suit himself.

After the chaos of the first session, other sessions were held in the Robing Room behind the great hall of the castle, a great number of English guards being placed on the door. The Maid was taken there by Jean Massieu who, sympathetic to the girl's plight, willingly agreed to let her kneel before the chapel as they passed. Whenever she did so, Jehanne devoutly bowed to the earth and made a prayer. Perhaps it shows you the malice of Lord Pig-Face and his pack of dogs; he was so displeased to hear of this action that he ordered Massieu not to allow the Maid to make this genuflection in future. In fact, one of Cauchon's greatest bastards, the prosecutor, D'Estivez, actually approached Massieu one evening when he was seated next to me in the castle hall.

'What makes you so bold as to allow this excommunicated whore to approach the church without permission? If you do it again, I will have you put in the tower where you will see neither moon nor sun.'

Massieu simply continued eating. D'Estivez glared at him, so I removed my knife from its sheath and placed it on the table in front of me. He glared once more at Massieu and then bustled out of the hall. A fat, evil man. I stared after him curiously. Something stirred and pricked my memory.

The sessions continued, with the questions so persistent that the Maid had to cry out:

'Sirs, one at a time, please. One at a time!'

Beaupere, one of Pig-Face's turds, even intervened

claiming he was the one supposed to ask the questions and would the others keep quiet. They tried to trap Jehanne on a number of things. First, she wore masculine attire, specifically condemned by the Book of Deuteronomy. The Maid's reply was tart:

'What I have done is by the commandment of God. If he had commanded me to take another dress I should have taken it because it would have been by God's command.'

As Massieu once said to me, when tipsy:

'How can anyone ride a horse wearing a dress? Anybody who went into battle would be forced, never mind God, to wear the same clothing the Maid had.'

Secondly, they concentrated on her voices, but the Maid proved her astonishing ability to fend off, and even contradict, some of the great legal minds of the day. One of the questions put to her:

'Does the voice wake you by touching your arm?'

This was a clever question posed in the hope that the Maid would say the saint made physical contact. She adroitly side-stepped it and replied:

'It woke me without touching me.'

Another series of questions followed:

*Questioner*: 'Did you see their faces?'

*The Maid*: 'Yes.'

*The Questioner persisted*: 'Have they any hair?'

*The Maid*: 'Yes. It is good to know they have.'

*Questioner*: 'Is their hair long and hanging down?'

*The Maid*: 'I don't know.'

*Questioner*: 'If they haven't limbs, how can they speak?'

*The Maid*: 'Ask God.'

*Questioner*: 'Does St. Margaret speak English?'

*The Maid*: 'Why should she speak English when she is not on the English side?'

*Questioner*: 'What did St. Michael look like when he appeared to you?'

*The Maid*: 'I know nothing about his garments.'

3. *The trial involved Charles of France but he was neither present nor represented.*

4. *No list of accusations had been given to the accused.*

The lawyer, therefore, thought the trial was invalid, refused Cauchon's invitation to join the Bishop's panel and immediately left Rouen.

Cauchon decided to drive a wedge between Jehanne and the Pope. On one occasion, the Maid was pressed to submit to the Church. She replied that she would willingly submit to the Holy Father and asked to be taken to him straight away.

I became so alarmed at the way the Maid was baiting her judges that I approached Massieu outside the chapel to speak to him.

'How do her replies seem to you, Jean? Will she be burnt? What will happen?'

Massieu looked at me sadly and tapped me gently on the shoulder.

'Up to now, I have seen nothing but good and honour in her and nothing reprehensible. Yet I do not know what will happen in the end. God knows.'

Eventually, Cauchon, concerned at the way the Maid was defending herself in public, decided the sessions would no longer be held even in the Robing Room. Instead, Jehanne would be confined to her cell and her interrogators would be sent there to continue their investigations. However, so stressful did this arrangement become that the Maid fell seriously ill and Cauchon ordered one of his assessors, who was also a doctor, to attend her. I later learnt from Massieu as to what happened. When the doctor was taken to the Maid he was accompanied by D'Estivez. When the Maid saw the latter, she flew into a rage, accusing the Bishop of Beauvais of sending her a poisoned carp. D'Estivez retorted by accusing her of eating herrings and other

*Questioner, in the hope of trapping the Maid into revealing some form of sexual misdemeanour*: 'Was he naked?'

*The Maid*: 'Do you think our Lord has nothing to dress him in?'

*Questioner*: 'Does he have any hair?'

*The Maid*: 'Who?'

*Questioner*: 'St. Michael.'

*The Maid*: 'Why? Should it have been cut off?'

Such humour often won the admiration of those persecuting and prosecuting her, especially when she became angry with them and threatened to box the ears of one of the notaries because of some mistake in the record. Then it was back to her dress again. The prosecutor put another question:

'Would you rather take women's clothing and hear Mass or retain your men's clothing and not hear it?'

The Maid replied: 'Guarantee that I shall hear it if I dress as a woman and then I will answer.'

It was tragic to hear the level of questioning about the voices and the woman's dress. The poor Maid did not realise that the more skilful and clever were her replies, the deeper she dug her own grave, for Cauchon was furious. He had expected the Maid to break, to convict herself out of her own mouth with heresy. Instead, all she was doing was astonishing some of the very people who wanted to send her to the stake. Indeed, there were even mutterings that things should be managed better. Cauchon even went to consult a well-respected priest and legal expert who had just arrived in Rouen. Cauchon gave him a copy of the trial minutes and asked for an opinion. When the priest returned, Cauchon was furious for the following points were made:

1. *The trial was irregular for it was being held in a closed and shut place in the castle.*

2. *Those present were not at liberty to give their real thoughts.*

things which she knew would disagree with her. I was alarmed when I heard this piece of news. Did the Maid consider suicide? The same thought had also occurred to those in charge of her. Another doctor was called in, Guillaume de la Chambre, who was brought before Beaufort and Warwick. The Earl spoke to him:

'I hear La Pucelle is ill, so we have sent for you to cure her. We do not want her to die a natural death for we hold her dear, having bought her dearly. She must die only at the hands of justice and must be burnt. Do whatever is necessary but restore her to health.' He also added a warning note. 'Be cautious of bloodletting. She is sly and might cause her own death.'

Once the Maid was better, the ordeal continued. Lent passed and Easter Sunday. She begged to hear Mass but they refused. I watched, almost with bated breath, and scoured the dining-hall, kitchens and servants' quarters to listen to gossip and piece bits together. I wondered when Beaufort would send for me. How could I effect the Maid's release? Of course, I might have tried to free her by myself but there again I might have been captured. I feared for Jehanne and hated what was being done, but I also had great care for my own welfare.

The macabre prosecution of the Maid was reaching its climax when Beaufort did eventually send for me. We met in a tavern in a narrow street off the market-place in Rouen. Beaufort had chosen the venue and came disguised in a heavy cloak with his head covered by a hood which he did not remove. On entering, I had great difficulty in finding him until I felt my sleeve being pulled. I turned, saw the cowled figure sitting in a dark corner, and recognised Beaufort. I smiled. If he was meeting me secretly he was going to make decisions independent of Warwick, Bedford and Cauchon, in this place where no spy or eavesdropper could listen in. I sat down and gazed around. Beaufort had chosen well; a low-ceilinged, black-timbered room with sawdust on the floor. The walls were lined with barrels and tables, which were simple trestles with planks across them, and a few stools. It was not a place to find a Cardinal of England in. I admired his courage. If any of the Armagnac faction had recognised him coming through the mud and mire of the streets, they would have killed him on the spot. Beaufort came swiftly to the point.

'The Maid,' he began in a hushed voice, 'must recant and abjure her errors.'

'In return for what?' I replied.

Beaufort looked up and grinned from his dark cowl.

'A sentence of perpetual imprisonment, of bitter bread and stale water, followed by a swift escape. There is a secret passageway beneath the cell. It can be arranged and you will ensure that it is carried out. But she must abjure! She must recant! You must persuade her to do that first, otherwise she is doomed!'

He hissed the last words and, before I could reply, rose to his feet and slipped out of the tavern.

The following day, I formally applied to Beaufort to see the Maid and he agreed. He despatched a writ saying I could meet her by myself just before vespers but the visit was to last no longer than half an hour. At the appointed time, I approached the Tour de Tresor and gained access to the Maid's cell. She was sitting on a straw-filled mattress with her hands and feet chained by thick, iron gyves. A metal coil around her waist was fastened to a huge beam which lay on the cell floor. The guards, when they saw Beaufort's writ, withdrew and I was alone with her. She looked pale and exhausted. Her face, usually thin, was now emaciated with great, dark circles under her eyes, yet when she saw me she smiled and tried to assert herself.

'For whatever reason you have come, Jankyn, it is not to torture, persecute or entrap me,' she said slowly. 'So,

why are you here?'
   'Your voices,' I began. 'Do they still speak to you?'
The Maid looked around at the dark, granite cell and
up at the heavy, black-beamed ceiling.
   'Yes, even in this dreadful place, they come to me.'
   'And what do they say?' I persisted.
   'They offer me hope. They say I may even escape.'
   'Are you sure?'
   'I am confident,' she replied. 'Is that why you are
here, Jankyn?'
   She seemed to read my thoughts. I made a gesture
with my hands for her to lower her voice. I knew that
there might well be peep-holes and pry-holes around
the wall for spies to listen in and report on what was
said.
   'You must abjure,' I said. 'You must recant and
perhaps it can be arranged.'
   The Maid looked away and stared down at a point
between her feet.
   'I cannot do that!' she replied hoarsely. 'It would be
wrong.'
   'No, it would not,' I insisted quietly. 'Any oath or
promise made under duress, even the Church says this,
would be wrong and invalid. If you do not abjure, you
might be tortured and burnt alive with your ashes being
strewn on the garbage heaps of the city.' For some
strange reason, perhaps a peasant's fear of an
unhallowed grave or the sheer degradation of her death
with the prospect of her body being dumped as a piece
of refuse, this alarmed the Maid. She asked me a
number of times if that would be the manner of her
death. I, of course, agreed there would be no
alternative. The Maid muttered that she would think
and pray about my suggestion. She lapsed into silence
with her chained hands resting on her knee. Then she
gestured for me to go and lay down on the mattress,
turning her face to the wall.

A few days later, I think it was the 8th May, a fine, warm day which made us realise spring had come and winter had died, the castle courtyard was sunny, smelling strongly as the piles of manure and refuse began to stink under the sun. At the same time, the strengthening breeze brought the smell of grass and blossom in from the surrounding fields. I remember it well. A stark contrast to what was happening in the castle. On the one hand, the deadly corruption and malevolence of Cauchon and his coven and, on the other, the Maid's simplicity in the face of horrible threats that she might be killed. Anyway, I ramble on. Strange, isn't it – when you are old your mind seems to want to remember what was the first day of spring or the first day the weather changed in years long past. But I remember that day well for they took the Maid out of her cell and down to the great dungeon of the castle to show her the instruments of torture. They threatened to inflict the strap, the water-boot and the rack if she would not abjure. They even took a vote, those nasty little turds, as to whether she would be tortured or not. One of them, some idiot, said she would be, for her own good! How evil can you get when a priest actually recommends that another human being should be tortured for their own good! Anyway, they put this offer to the Maid and, of course, she just laughed at them and told them to do their worst. They didn't, not out of charity or compassion but because Warwick sent an order down that the Maid was not to be tortured. She was to be reserved for a greater show and, who knows, that might be spoilt if she died in her agonies. They threatened to burn her but she replied that she would not change her attitude even if she was to see the fire lighted. She added that even if she was actually in the fire she would sustain everything she had said to the bitter end.

This was enough for Cauchon. Two weeks later, on

the 24th May, she was taken out to the walled cemetery adjoining the Abbey of St. Ouen. I followed the procession, lines and phalanxes of men-at-arms wearing the surcoats of Warwick and the royal arms of England. They crowded round the two carts, one carrying the Maid and the other the executioner. He was stark and grim, with his eyes glittering through the slits in the black hood, sombrely dressed in his red jerkin and hose thrust into black leather riding-boots. The instruments of torture lay around him in the cart. Sword, axe, firebrand and tinder, they were the symbols of the State's power and its ability to inflict horrific death. The English court also went along, bloody Warwick, Beaufort, Stafford and other leading notables. I, too, was there with my excitement so intense I found it difficult at times to control my breathing. The previous evening, just before midnight, Beaufort had allowed me to see the Maid again privately. I had warned her, they were going to take her out and read the admonition. Unless she abjured there, in the walled cemetery of St. Ouen, they would hand her over to the State executioner to be burnt alive. For the first and only time in my life, I saw the Maid frightened. She said she would think about my promise and, just as I was about to rise and leave, she spoke almost as an afterthought.

'Tell my Lord Cardinal to have the abjuration ready and I may well sign it.'

# SEVENTEEN

I waited to see what would happen. Would the Maid remain stubborn or would she accept and grasp the one offer of escape and freedom? The whole city of Rouen had turned out to watch the spectacle, with huge crowds on either side of the main thoroughfare. As the procession passed, they packed in behind, following us down until all around the abbey there was a huge sea of faces. The procession finally made its way into the wide, cobbled market-place of Rouen. Overlooking the square were the great black and white timbered houses of the merchants who had their stalls and booths beneath in an arcade. The square was packed and the crowd pressed in on ranks of soldiers six deep, who kept the central place clear for the two large scaffolds. One scaffold was for Beaufort, Beauvais and the others and on the other scaffold was the executioner with Jehanne who was dressed in a simple white shift.

The process was begun whereby the Maid would be publicly admonished to abjure her errors. This was to be done by some theologian from Paris. I forget the prick's name but he later confessed he would have preferred to be in Flanders rather than to have carried out the task assigned to him. I climbed on to the scaffold where Beaufort was sitting, telling the guards and tipstaffs that I was of the Cardinal's household and wanted to be next to him. This caused a stir. I saw Beaufort turn and nod. I was let through and stood behind him just as the priest on the other scaffold began a long, boring sermon. Something about everyone being a branch of a tree and if a branch was diseased it should be cut off. It was the usual rubbish priests come out with when they try to admonish someone.

I looked around and could see a few rotten branches I would have liked to lop off. The Maid simply stood there looking out over the crowd which, as the sermon become more lengthy and complicated, grew restive. Some refuse was thrown and there were shouts at them.

'Get on with it! Burn the witch! Shut the priest up!'

The preacher happily obliged by speaking faster, as if he wished to get through his prepared text and be gone. At the end, he viciously attacked King Charles and was cut short by the Maid proclaiming that *he* was the liar and that the French King was a good Christian. The preacher shouted back at Massieu, who was on the platform next to the Maid, to shut the French whore up but Massieu just shrugged. The Maid laughed out loud and my heart warmed to her bravery.

Henry VI's secretary, Lawrence Callott, suddenly rose from his seat next to Beaufort, went down across the square and on to the scaffold. The preacher took that as a sign that the sentence should be carried out. A deadly hush fell upon the crowd as the preacher, now in measured and solemn tones, began to intone the decree of excommunication:

'For these reasons mentioned before, the Church decrees you, Jehanne, excommunicate and heretical and pronounces that you should be abandoned to secular justice as a limb of Satan severed from the Church.'

I watched the Maid, after weeks of strong resolution, hear those dreadful words rolling out like drumbeats. She gazed wildly round at the executioner, now standing upright in his cart, and at the upturned faces of the cruel, rapacious crowd. She slumped on the stool

and cried out that she would defer. She would abjure. I
sprang to my feet but a low growl broke from the crowd
as if they sensed they would be deprived of seeing the
Maid burnt. My memory is confused. I heard the Maid
call upon St. Michael and I looked back to where
Jehanne stood. Callot had taken a small document out
of his sleeve and I knew Beaufort must have had it
ready for the Maid to sign. The Maid shouted at Callott:

'I know neither how to read or write!'

Callott clasped her fingers round the pen and,
guiding her hand, drew a round 'O' and then another
sign. I forget what it was. Callott held the document up.

'The Maid has abjured!' he cried. 'She has renounced
her heresies, her sorcery and her work for the upstart
calling himself Charles VII of France!'

The Maid interrupted him saying that she was
confused, so Massieu, out of pity, took the document
from Callott's hand and read it to her. The crowd's
murmur turned into a roar and stones were thrown.
Lord Pig-Face angrily turned to where Beaufort was
sitting. He shouted at someone, I do not know whether
it was at Beaufort or somebody else:

'You will pay for this! I have been insulted! I will not
proceed until I have been satisfied!'

Beaufort, the expert liar and debater, immediately
replied:

'Cauchon, it is you who are favouring the Maid!'

'You lie!' Cauchon shouted, and standing up, threw
his papers angrily to the ground saying he would go no
further that day.

Over on the scaffold on which the Maid stood, there
was confusion. I heard the Maid laugh. Someone read
the document out again and the Maid shouted out:

'I have signed! I have signed! Are you not satisfied?'

Lord Pig-Face, now recovering his temper, realised
that he had insulted the Cardinal in public. He turned
to Beaufort and bitterly asked what he should do next.

Beaufort shrugged and smiled.

'She is penitent, my Lord Bishop,' he replied, 'so accept her as a penitent.'

Pig-Face licked his lips, took deep breaths to control the temper which must have been raging inside him. In a short, staccato sermon, shouted in defiance at the crowd (which was now hurling insults as well as anything else they could get their hands on), he declared the Maid was released from the threat of excommunication and was admitted once more to the bosom of Mother Church. However, she was to be condemned to perpetual imprisonment and to the bread of pain and the water of sorrow so that she might expiate her faults to the end of her days. Loiselleur, like some cur sensing the changing mood of its masters, got up and approached the edge of the scaffold on which Cauchon stood. He shouted across to the Maid.

'Jehanne, you have spent a good day. Please God, you have saved your soul!'

The Maid ignored him but shouted back at the rest:

'If you are men of the Church, you have got what you want. Return me to the prison!'

The journey back to the castle was confusing and tumultuous. The Maid was insulted by the English soldiers, with their officers doing nothing to stop them. In fact, Beaufort had been clever in passing the blame on to Cauchon; Warwick and others were now very indignant with the Bishop of Beauvais because the Maid had not been pronounced guilty, condemned and given up for execution. So intense was this ill-feeling against them that when Cauchon and his company returned to the castle, some English guards drew their swords and lowered their pikes as if to attack. They shouted that Cauchon had ill-earned the English King's money.

Inside the castle yard, where the leaders, Beaufort included, were grouped together almost shouting at each other, Warwick turned to Cauchon and bellowed at him:

'Our King is ill-served! The Maid is escaping!'

I do not know what Cauchon replied but it could have been thus:

'My Lord, do not worry! We will catch her again.'

Beaufort apparently heard the reply for he beckoned me to join him and whispered that I should meet him in his chamber as soon as he had left the castle yard. I found the Cardinal seated on a bench with a goblet of wine cradled between his hands. He looked up and I noticed how tired and drawn was his face.

'Close the door, Jankyn,' he said. 'Come here.' When I approached, he stared for a long while at me. 'You must leave now, Jankyn.' He delved into the deep pockets of his robe and drew out a purse of gold and a small leather packet. 'Take a horse, a sumpter pony and your belongings. Do not talk to anyone. Do not refer to the Maid. Do not even try and see her. You are to go to Calais, to a tavern called "The Hawthorn Bush". You are to deliver this sealed packet to the landlord. Tell him to expect a visitor in the very near future, a woman. He is to take her further up the coast, open this packet and follow the directions contained therein. You must not open this packet, Jankyn. You swear?'

'You have my word, my Lord. And the Maid?'

Beaufort just glared at me. 'I have told you once not to mention her name,' he muttered. 'Now go, before I change my mind.'

Exhausted after the day's events, I nevertheless obeyed. I threw my meagre belongings into saddle-bags and, using the Cardinal's name, secured horse and pack-pony from the stables. Within the hour, I was through the main gate of Rouen following the Seine north to Calais. It took me three days to get there and once I had delivered the message I journeyed back to Rouen. I had been gone for about seven days but as soon as I approached the walls of the city I sensed something was wrong. An atmosphere of subdued

terror, of menace, of spent anger; of something public
and, once done, all the people concerned, whether they
were implicated or not, felt guilty. I panicked, wanting
to spur my horse through the narrow lanes and streets
of Rouen to reach the castle. I controlled my breathing,
steadied my horse and made my way through the main
gateway and up into the square. Last time, it had been
packed with people surrounding the scaffolds watching
the Maid abjure and recant. Now, the square was empty
except for a great scaffold in the middle with a
blackened pillar high on a mound. The awful, sombre
stink of death filled the market-place. I looked around.
The merchants in their beaver hats, the artisans, the
townspeople, they were all subdued and unable to catch
each other's eye as if they suffered from that terrible
exhaustion which follows a public bloodletting. I wanted
to scream out. I wanted to shout. I wanted to ask
questions. Instead, I dismounted and like a shadow, a
ghost, passed amongst them into the castle.

Here, too, the same atmosphere filled the castle yard.
A few men passed and looked strangely at me. I gave
my horse over to some groom. I wanted to see Beaufort.
The Maid had been killed and I wished to control
neither my rage nor fury which made my heart pound
and the blood bang in my head. I went up to Massieu's
chamber on the second floor of the great donjon and
found him slouched on a stool in a corner already
half-drunk. He looked blearily at me as I entered,
smiled the half-vacuous grin of the toper, splashed wine
into a cup and held it out to me.

'Come in, Jankyn,' he said. 'You missed the end of the
hunt, the great kill, the death of the arch-fiend and the
enemy of Bedford and Warwick. The Maid is dead.'

I knew that already but his words almost stopped my
heart. A sweat broke out all over my body. I took the
wine and pulled a stool across to sit opposite him.

'What happened?' I muttered.

Massieu looked at me.

'What happened?' he said thickly. 'The bastards burnt her.'

'But she abjured. She was safe!'

'Oh, yes.' Massieu nodded. 'She was safe until Warwick had all that changed. The soldiers in the garrison here were very angry the Maid had not been burnt. They took it out on Cauchon's jackals whenever they turned up.' He looked up and blinked the tears away from his eyes. 'Anyway, they took away her boy's clothing, put it in a sack and she donned a dress. I believe she was abused by some of the guards but on Pentecost Sunday she rose and asked to go to the garde de robe.' Massieu concentrated to jog his memory. 'The guards had removed her woman's clothing and the only clothing they would give her was the boy's. At first, she refused this male attire. Eventually, because she wished to leave the bed for the purposes of nature, she put the clothing on, protesting as she did so,"Sirs, you know that this is forbidden but I cannot take it off without falling into fault". Once she was in male attire, a message was sent to Cauchon to say that the prisoner had defaulted. He visited her on the following Monday morning. She protested, accusing Cauchon of attempting to murder her but he said she was a recidivist going back to her old ways like a dog to its vomit.' Massieu licked his lips and drank a gulp of wine. 'Cauchon also asked her if she had heard the voices. She said "yes" and that they had been angry with her for her abjuration. That was all the old bastard needed. The following morning, he reconvened his assessors in the Archbishop's chapel. Forty-one opinions were asked. Forty-one were given. The Maid was a relapsed heretic, a recidivist, and she should be abandoned to secular justice with the request that they act mercifully towards her.' Massieu spat on the ground. 'You know what they meant by "mercifully". They meant "kill her". The next morning, on the 30th May, at seven in the morning, I returned to the Maid's room. I read out Cauchon's summons to appear at the Place de Vieille Marche in Rouen to be declared a heretic and excommunicate by the Church. I was joined by two friars and then read out the sentence of death. The Maid slumped to her knees crying out, "Alas, how can you treat me so cruelly? Is it really necessary that my body, so clean and complete and never sullied, should be consumed by flames and reduced to ashes? I would prefer to be seven times decapitated than burnt." The Maid stopped shouting and began to cry, hiding her face in her hands and clutching her hair.' Massieu stopped talking to brush tears from his eyes.

'And then what?' I asked softly.

'The Maid said these words. "I cry to God, the great judge, to behold the great injustices done to me." One of the friars heard her confession and, having gained permission from Cauchon, gave her communion. Cauchon entered the cell again. I heard the Maid cry out to him: "Bishop, I am dying because of you!" Then everyone withdrew. An hour later, the Maid was taken from the cell. Her grief was so great that she was beyond recognition. Her face was hooded and she had been dressed in a long, grey-black dress which had been coated with sulphur and pitch up to the neck. She was taken to the castle yard, lifted into a cart and we joined her there. The Maid seemed listless and tired. We went, escorted by about one hundred and twenty soldiers, through the cobbled streets to the Vieille Marche. The place had been cleared. About eight hundred of Warwick's soldiers guarded the streets leading into the market-place, so sealing off all access to it. These streets were packed with onlookers. There were three scaffolds erected. One was for the judges, including Cauchon, another for the secular authorities, and on the third, where the executioner stood, a special pillar with wood and plaster stacked around it. It had been erected high above the ground but partially hidden by a large notice.' Massieu bit his lip. 'On this were lies about the Maid.' He closed his eyes to remember. 'Jehanne, who calls herself "The Maid" – liar, pernicious deceiver of the people, sorceress, superstitious blasphemer of God, presumptuous disbeliever of the faith in Jesus Christ, braggart, idolatrous, cruel, wanton, invoker of the Devil, apostate, schismatic and heretic.' Massieu sipped from his wine-cup before continuing, 'The Maid had to listen to Cauchon and someone else giving a long sermon. She was then handed over to the secular arm. Her moans were something terrible. They placed a mitre on her head, forcing it down over the hood. This, too, bore inscriptions of what she had done. The Maid was seized and tied in the middle of the pyre. The executioner set fire to the wood. I saw flame burst out of a massive pall of smoke. I heard the Maid cry out a few times and then her head slumped forward. At this point, the crowds were allowed to come forward from the streets. The executioner pulled aside some of the faggots so that we saw the half-charred body of a woman. The fire was then built up again and the corpse was consumed.'

Massieu bit his lip and took a long drink from his cup. 'Your Bishop Beaufort ordered that the ashes be placed in a sack and thrown into the Seine. So,' he concluded hoarsely, 'the Maid is dead!'

# EIGHTEEN

I just could not believe it. I sat and watched this small, fat priest, drunk to the point of idiocy, tell me in short, sharp phrases how the Maid had died. Her death would have been quick. She would have been choked on the smoke, the sulphur on the dress would have seen to that. A terrible rage seethed through me. Beaufort had promised the Maid would live and yet she had been taken out and executed in a barbaric way. I got up, knocking the stool away from me, and strode out of Massieu's room straight to Beaufort's chamber in the Tour de Tresor. I burst into his room, knocking aside secretaries and even an armed guard. Beaufort was seated behind his desk carefully studying some manuscript. As I came in, I noticed alarm in his eyes and saw his hand go beneath the table where I knew he must keep some dagger.

'Jankyn,' he said, 'you did what I asked?'

'Yes,' I shouted out, 'and you, you sanctimonious bastard, did you do what you promised?'

Beaufort got up. The urgency and speed of his movement calmed me. He walked over to the door and closed it, shouting at his servants that he was in no danger and they were to leave him. He turned and, leaning against the door, looked steadily at me.

'So you think the Maid died?'

'Of course the Maid died!' I retorted. 'Massieu, who had been with her throughout the trial, saw her loaded

179

on to the cart. You cannot escape from a pyre dressed in a coat of sulphur!'

'Massieu,' the Bishop replied, 'saw a woman die.' He walked over to me. 'Listen Jankyn, he saw a woman die.'

'Are you saying,' I said slowly, 'that the Maid did not die in the market-place of Rouen?'

Beaufort smiled. 'The Maid has gone. Her ashes are in the Seine. Who would believe her now?'

'But you promised,' I said. 'You promised the Maid her life, to deprive the Armagnacs of a martyr. Now she is dead and I am partly responsible for it. So are you. Her blood is on our hands.'

I suppose I have never really felt kinship with anyone in the Gospels, but the words were scarcely out of my mouth when I felt an empathy with Judas throwing down the blood-money in the temple. Beaufort stared at me.

'Listen!' he said. 'A woman, cloaked and hooded, was taken out of Beaurevoir Castle and carried to the execution square where the crowd were not allowed to see her. There she was put into a pyre of faggots which were built up around her and so she died. Do you understand what I am saying, Jankyn?' He flicked a finger towards the door. 'I have always admired you for your brain and your sharp sense. Go and think about what I have said. Ask whatever questions you may but be very careful, Jankyn. The public truth is that the Maid is dead! Get out!'

I got up and walked away. I knew what Beaufort was telling me. He loved that sort of game where everything shone in mirrors; nothing substantial, nothing real, but always a reflection of what might be or should be. Was he saying that the Maid had survived? Had he brought about her escape? I went to my own quarters and hid, like a hermit, to think very carefully about what Beaufort had said. Firstly, it was strange how the square had been cleared of townspeople. Secondly, I knew canon law. I had studied at Oxford and had seen executions. The prisoner was always taken out with head and face exposed so that the clergy could preach to the faithful and point to the dangers of the sin of heresy and schism. So why was the Maid cloaked and hooded?

After a number of solitary days of sitting, eating, drinking and thinking, I decided to make my own enquiries. I went back to Massieu.

'You are sure,' I asked him, 'that you were on the scaffold with the Maid?'

'Why, yes of course,' he said. I noticed his eyes were still red and puffy through too much drink and crying.

'And the Maid. How did she act?'

'Quietly,' Massieu said. 'She was quiet and withdrawn, though sometimes she prayed. She seemed to be waiting for something though I am not sure for what. I never really saw her face once we left the castle.'

I uttered my thanks and went down to the city. I gained directions from one of Cauchon's assessors about the whereabouts of Godfrey Forseiger, the chief executioner of Rouen. I found him, a bland-eyed, moon-faced killer with black, greasy hair in ringlets, sitting outside a tavern enjoying the summer sun. He was a solitary man with a reputation of being so ferocious that people avoided him and the stink of death which always surrounded him. I introduced myself, bought him a drink and sat down, both of us watching two children digging in the sewer which ran down the middle of the street.

'Were you responsible for the execution of the Maid?' I began.

Forseiger nodded. 'Why?'

'There was nothing strange?'

'Nothing,' he said.

'Did the Maid say anything?'

'A number of times she cried out the name "Jesus" but

nothing else,' Forseiger said, pursing his fat lips in thought. 'She was a schismatic, a sorceress, and she died.'

'Why did you pull aside the faggots? I asked.

'So the half-charred body could be seen by the crowd,' Forseiger answered. 'Beaufort, your own master, told me to do that. "You are to make sure that the people see the Maid is dead." You see, the Maid was not burnt at the stake but in the pyre.' Forseiger took a cup and turned it upside down so it rested with its rim against the table-top. 'She was tied to a pillar and the faggots were built up around her. I went in to make sure that she was fast against the pole, came out, filled the gap with brushwood and then lit some wet straw. The whole thing exploded in smoke.'

'But surely,' I said, 'you often show mercy to the prisoners by going in and strangling them before the flames reach them?'

Forseiger nodded. 'Of course, but in this case the flames were too intense. Moreover, she must have died in seconds. Why do you want to know?' he asked.

'For nothing,' I replied slowly. 'I watched her trial and I wanted to know how she died.' I then rose and left him.

The next few days I spent touring the prisons, talking to greasy-aproned gaolers about who had been held therein and taking a particular interest in any women arrested for sorcery. In one, a small bastille at the other end of the city, I found the gaoler to be evasive and unable to produce lists. Another piece of the puzzle fell into place. I went back to the castle and revisited the cell in which the Maid had been held. Nobody bothered to stop me. I felt sad and desolate. Now that the Maid was gone, there was no reason for security or guards. It was a sad, pathetic sight. I saw the wooden beam with the chain still attached to it and the bed with the straw mattress still pressed down in the shape of the Maid's body. A cracked pewter cup lay under the bed, together with two sticks which had once formed a cross. Scratches were on the walls where the Maid had attempted to keep some idea of the passage of time in the agony of the days. There was a quiet desolation about the place.

I checked the walls and the floor but nothing moved. There were no secret compartments. I remembered what Beaufort had said about secret tunnels and took a closer look at the passageways around the cell and the stairwells leading up through the tower. I went down to the entrance and noticed that there were two, almost parallel, passages separated by a small recess. On the left, the entrance led to a drawbridge which linked the tower to the interior court of the castle. The right one led to a landing, preceded by two steps, which led to the cell where the Maid had been kept. The passage then continued on to a spiral staircase which went up to the first floor. There, just inside the doorway to the cell from the passage, I found a small, very dark recess and in it a well-oiled, square trapdoor which, when pulled back, revealed a flight of steps leading down to a passage which must run right under the castle into the fields beyond.

That night, I had the strangest of dreams, constantly plagued by what had happened to the Maid. My fevered mind and evil humour took me back to her cell and I watched, as in a trance, to what might have happened on the morning of Wednesday, the 30th May. I saw the Maid talking to Cauchon, the two friars hearing her confession and giving the Sacrament before withdrawing. Beaufort entered the room and the chain was removed. The Maid slipped out into the dark recess and Beaufort allowed her to go down through the trapdoor into the passage and freedom. Some other woman, a convicted sorceress, who had been heavily drugged and given false promises, was substituted for the Maid. Wrapped in a cloak and hood, this woman was taken to the Vieille Marche area. Still cloaked and hooded, she was imprisoned in the pyre of faggots and burnt to death. Beaufort ensured the body was displayed to the public and whatever ashes remained were thrown into the Seine.

When I awoke, I remember swinging my legs off the bed and walking furiously up and down the room wondering if my dream reflected the truth. If so, it had been a brilliant plan. Beaufort had seized the Maid, using me to trap her and bring her to Rouen. He fully intended to kill her but later changed his mind. Why should he provide the Armagnacs with a martyr, some saint to rally behind? Why should he do La Tremoille's dirty work and that of the other ministers of Charles VII? Why should Beaufort, a man of the Church, a priest, have the blood of such a woman upon his hands? But, I thought, the world believed the Maid had died at the stake so Beaufort would still receive the blame even if the Maid had escaped. Then I saw the real beauty and the sheer simplicity of his brilliant plan. I knew what would happen. If the Maid re-emerged, people would be divided. Some would say she was an imposter and others that she had collaborated with the English and abjured her errors. Anyway, who would trust her? At the same time, if she remained silent and hidden, Beaufort would have achieved his end without committing murder and he wouldn't care a fig about anything else. Beaufort, in fact, would love the situation. Only he would know the truth. Whichever way the Maid moved, Beaufort would still control the game. As in chess, however the pieces were moved, Beaufort would win.

The following evening, I returned to the Tour de Tresor and sat in the Maid's cell. I got up and walked over to one of the windows and looked out at the green fields which the tower overlooked. Across them, at some time early on Wednesday, the 30th May, the Maid had

walked to freedom and I wondered where she was and
what she was doing. I also realised why I had been
involved in this mystery and why I had stayed caught in
Beaufort's snare. What attachment had I, an Englishman and a coward, for the Maid? I suppose it was quite
simple. In my long and sinful life, I believe she was the
nearest I have ever come to God.

I can see that the stupid priest who is taking this down
now looks at me in surprise. Like all his kind, the
English clerical and lay, both estates, believe the Maid
was a heretic and a sorceress who died in Rouen. He is
wrong. Over the years, I have collected evidence. There
was a Dean of Metz who maintained the Maid
reappeared in France in 1435. Other rumours claim the
Maid joined her two brothers, Pierre and Jacques, in
Lorraine five years after she was supposedly burnt at
the stake. There is even evidence that Charles VII met
this person claiming to be the Maid and accepted her as
such, allowing her to marry one of his noblemen,
Robert des Armoises.

It is true the Maid did not take a leading part in the
war but why should she? You see, Beaufort had made
one mistake. He believed the Maid could be kept
incarcerated whilst the English regained their triumphs
in France. Why not? They had done so for fifteen years
before the Maid's appearance. Beaufort reached the
logical conclusion that once the Maid was out of the way
England would regain its footing. This was not so.
Burgundy threw in his lot with France. The same year
the Maid reappeared in France, 1435, saw the Treaty of
Arras which marked the beginning of the end of
English fortunes in France.

Perhaps that is why Charles VII did nothing for the
Maid, because he knew she had been returned into
French keeping. Perhaps Beaufort had made some
secret pact with the French about the Maid being
detained for a while in return for her life. It is strange

that King Charles did nothing until 1450 when he entered Rouen, two years after, so my spies said, the Maid is supposed to have died, honoured and loved as the Lady des Armoises. After he re-entered the city, he staged a rehabilitation trial for Jehanne, but you should know by now that you cannot trust everything you hear.

Oh, I know that old bastard. Cauchon, who died so suddenly, had minutes and a record kept of the trial which sent Jehanne the Maid to the stake, but very few people realised how it took him six months to edit the text. It can be trusted as much as a bucket with a hole. As far as the rehabilitation trial is concerned, well I have seen some of the documents and heard some of the stories. They are really a joke. I mean, Frenchmen, who had co-operated with the English occupiers in killing Jehanne, had to account for their actions. Of course, they all brought forward marvellous stories of how they had really sympathised with her and cried when she died. I tell you something. If Cauchon's record is faulty, the rehabilitation trial is the next best thing to whitewashing a dirty pigsty. I mean, when you get men like Godfrey Forseiger, the Rouen executioner who placed the faggots around the stake and lit them, actually claiming how he saw white doves leaving the pyre as she died! That her entrails refused to burn! Gods, if you think this is true you will believe anything! Perhaps it is a sign of the times, the absolute decay of morals, that you cannot put any credence on what you read. What is the world coming to?

Of course, I did think of going back to that inn on the Normandy coast and enquiring about who had arrived there, but I dare not. I had given Beaufort my word and I could not renege on it. Instead I collected bits of evidence: the execution book of Rouen does not mention Joan's death; in 1439 Jehanne, the Maid, (now Jehanne Armoise), was entertained and accepted by Jacques Boucher who had sheltered both her and me ten years earlier at Orleans. The same city also voted their favourite daughter supplies in recompense for what she had done.

Oh, many's the time I thought of going across to see her but I could not. What would happen if I was wrong? I'm such a cynic. Joan the Maid is one of the few beacons in my sensuous existence. I could not tolerate meeting some dupe, a stupid girl playing a sick, dangerous game. I was content, nay, even revelled in the thought of Jehanne's escape. So why should I have the cup dashed from my lips? I made my decision and stood by it in 1431 when I left Rouen, convinced the Maid had escaped. Oh, by the way, never once, in his long career, did Beaufort ever raise, or allow me to raise, the subject of the Maid. True, I often wondered what his role in saving the Maid had been. Years after Beaufort's death, a pilgrim told me that when passing through the Chapel of St. Joan in La Turbie, a mountain village near Nice in Southern France, he found a ring with the words 'Jesu Maria' engraved on it. The very ring the Maid had worn. According to an inscription, the Maid had given it to Beaufort who, in turn, had presented it to the church. Perhaps only I know the reason for Beaufort's gift.

Oh, yes, I was finished with Rouen except for one thing. I remembered D'Estivez threatening Massieu. Something in his voice had stirred a memory, so I spent two days following him and Loiselleur around Rouen. They still strutted about, full of their own importance. One night I heard them in a tavern; usually they spoke in hushed voices but D'Estivez made the mistake of laughing and I knew these two turds were the Shadows. After that it was simple. I hired a number of bully-boys, a group of burly Yorkshire archers, plied them with drink, gave them some money and jogged their memories about how Cauchon and his priests had nearly allowed the Maid to escape.

I told them what I wanted and promised them more gold once the deed was carried out. Both Loiselleur and D'Estivez spent weeks recovering in the infirmary of a local monastery from the appalling injuries sustained in a sudden and vicious attack upon them whilst walking through the streets of Rouen. I did consider visiting them for the care of the sick is a corporal act of mercy. Yet, time was short so I sent them an anonymous message – 'Those acts done in the shadows shall one day be judged in the light.' I thought it was a nice little gesture. I am sure the bastards never forgot me!

I also sent some gold to the widow in Orleans, God bless her! The little priest who is transcribing this has tears in his eyes. Lord above, he is a stupid bastard! He moons over me, accepts my insults, just because I sent money to his family and built a house for his mother. If he does not stop bothering me, I will send men down to burn the place around the old crone's ears! Once, when I helped some orphan children, he wanted to put up a small statue in my name in the church. I told the silly rat's-bottom that if he did anything like that I would hang him over his own bloody sanctuary!

Ah well, as I said, I left Rouen and came home. The years have passed and I look back on those times; hard men, fierce days. Not like now, the youths are soft, drink too much, eat too much; far too much dicing, too much wenching. They are even printing books now, a sure sign of the decline in morals. All done by that William Caxton at his shop under the Red Sign near Westminster, books for people to read. Where will it all end? I mean, you shouldn't believe everything you read. Lord save us, the collapse of morals! The Maid has gone. I miss her. Soon I will follow. Sweet Jesus, I wonder where Beaufort is?

# Author's Note

Jankyn is a liar. Indeed, a prince amongst liars. We do not know if he even went to France, though his description of the Maid, her campaigns and the politics of the time is particularly accurate. There were very strong rumours that the Maid did survive her death and escaped from the pyre. Several historians have successfully argued that, given the details of her execution, especially her face being hooded in the cart, and the way she was fastened to the stake concealed within bundles of faggots, it could be possible. A woman later claiming to be Joan, whose claims were supported by Joan's own brother, did emerge some years later. Beaufort's role in her trial was also curious. He did not intervene but was seen to cry when the pyre was lit. Surprisingly, he was the one who gave the order for the Maid's ashes to be thrown into the Seine. More interestingly still, he did have one of the Maid's rings and later presented it to a church as a gift. We shall never know the real truth.

As for Jankyn's claims? According to his voluminous confession, Jankyn turns up in a great deal of the political mischief in 15th century England. The author cannot be held responsible for his continued outrageous claims!